WINTER WISHES

WINTER WITCHES OF HOLIDAY HAVEN

ELLE ADAMS

This book was written, produced and edited in the UK, where some spelling, grammar and word usage will vary from US English.

Copyright © 2020 Elle Adams
All rights reserved.

To be notified when Elle Adams's next book is released, sign up to her author newsletter.

Hark! The Herald

Volume No. 352   Editor Archer Olsen   December 18, 2020

Rudolph Missing! Jack Frost wanted for questioning in connection to the reindeer-napping.

All of Holiday Haven and the North Pole are on the lookout for the missing reindeer. Police say to be alert for a shiny red nose. Some have even said it glows. All of the other reindeer are highly concerned and want their front runner returned safely. Citizens worry about toy delivery delays without Rudolph to light the way. Will Santa be able to see his way through a snow storm without Rudolph and his mighty nasal superpower? Experts say it's unlikely. If you have any information on Rudolph's location or Jack Frost's whereabouts, inform your local police.

Is Christmas Canceled? Heinous Hex stops toy production at Toy Workshop.

Who could be behind the dastardly deed? Who in all of Holiday Haven and the North Pole would want to keep toys from reaching all the good girls and boys in the world? Children full of questions for Santa. If not enough toys can be produced in time for Christmas, how will it be determined who gets toys? Some kind of points system? Santa could not be reached for comment.

Murder rocks the Christmas Market! Cursed cocoa linked to illegal potions ring.

Trouble at the Holiday Haven Inn? Mishaps and magical mayhem threaten to disrupt five-year anniversary celebration.

Santa's Sleigh Stolen: Is Christmas in jeopardy? Workshop security baffled and elves in disarray!

1

The Holiday Haven Inn was open for business, and we were always ready for the occasion.

I stood on a stepladder, affixing a banner over the door to the hall, which said, "Five Years of Festive Cheer." Genuine snowflakes drifted from the ceiling, while the large Christmas tree in the corner remained up all year round, decorated with glittering baubles. Snow dusted the front desk of the reception area, tinsel adorned the windowsills, and everything sparkled with festivity.

This weekend marked five years since my best friend and I had flown—literally—up to the North Pole to start anew in Holiday Haven, so we'd opted to host a major event to celebrate.

Perhaps we'd gone a little overboard with the decorations, but everyone in Holiday Haven knew how to get into the spirit of the season. In an enchanted town where Christmas was celebrated every day, no matter the time of year, you kind of had to.

Behind the desk, Mercy hung up the phone, tucking a

strand of her curly dark hair behind her ear. A thick red scarf was wrapped around her neck, matching the rest of her red-and-white ensemble, and she came over to join me next to the stepladder I stood on in order to reach the right spot above the door and finish putting the banner into place. "Nice job, Carol."

"Thanks." I smiled up at the glittering banner, which I'd spelled so that the letters glowed in the dark. I rarely used those spells these days, but it was one of the more useful skills I'd inherited from my parents. Possibly the only one, in fact. Entrepreneurial spirit ran in my family, too, but it'd been Mercy who'd masterminded our whole scheme to move to the North Pole to begin with. Even *that* sounded saner than some of the schemes my family had come up with, including the part where we'd moved into an abandoned shack and converted it into an inn for guests from out of town. But we'd built a successful business over the past five years, and I allowed myself a moment of pride for what we'd accomplished.

Despite appearances, it wasn't my festive name which had contributed to our decision to move here. I might not have wintery magic like Mercy did, but I loved the Christmas holidays. Always had. Not the damp and drizzly winters we got back in England, but the sort with actual snow and enough of it to build a village of snowmen and go sledging or ice skating every weekend. Holiday Haven had all that and more.

"I sorted out the ads," Mercy said. "We have a double-page spread in the papers, and we'll be on the front page of *Hark! The Herald* tomorrow."

"Awesome," I said. "What about the entertainment? Did the carollers get back to you?"

"They did," she said. "As expected, they said yes right away. Let's face it, they'll perform to an audience of inanimate snowmen if nobody else is around. Anyway, they've agreed to sing during the interludes of the play and to stand outside while we're welcoming people inside."

"Perfect." We'd also successfully convinced the town's biggest theatre company to put on an exclusive performance at the inn this upcoming Saturday. They'd been rehearsing for weeks, and while we'd hit a few minor hitches in the process, we'd also sold half the tickets already. Adding the town's enthusiastic carollers to our program would only increase the appeal.

A flutter of wings sounded when a large owl swooped through the window and dropped off a package in the reception area before departing the inn.

"Expecting a delivery?" I asked.

"Yes." She scooted over to the door and retrieved the square package before setting it down on the desk. Then she undid several layers of secure wrapping to reveal a smaller box inset with glittering gemstones and with a narrow slot in the side.

I studied the box when she held it up to show me. "Am I supposed to know what that is?"

"You know how we had trouble figuring out how to make everyone happy with the presents in Santa's grotto?" she asked, her blue eyes twinkling. "This is a genuine wishing box."

"Seriously?" I asked. "Where'd you find it?"

"I ordered it from a specialist shop back home in England. Took me long enough to find one." She placed the box onto the desk again. "I've never used one before, but I'm told it's fairly straightforward. Anyone who wants to use the box just needs to write their wish on a piece of paper and then put it into the box. Then it works its magic, and…" She snapped her fingers, and a few snowflakes drifted down onto the desk.

"Wow," I said. "Can you literally ask the box for anything?"

"Within reason. I was going to give it a test run first."

"Wise idea. I mean, what happens if a kid wishes they owned a giant robot dinosaur? That could get weird pretty fast."

Her brow crinkled. "Good point."

"We can't control what people wish for, either," I added. "Like if someone wishes the sky was green, or that we all lived underwater… would the box try to make that happen?"

"We can work from a list instead. The kids will ask for toys, while the adults will ask for fancy cars or houses…"

My brows shot up. "Do we want random houses falling out of the sky?" As for cars, sledges were the favoured mode of transport here in Holiday Haven, and for good reason. The ever-present snow on the roads all year round made driving a risky venture.

"Um…" She looked at the box dubiously. "Good point. I *think* it works by adjusting the circumstances so you end up with what you wish for, but there must be a limit somewhere."

"Not that I'm trying to dampen your idea," I added hastily. "Just thinking ahead in case someone decides to wish for something inadvisable and all hell breaks loose."

The last thing we needed was for our weekend celebration to be derailed if someone decided to wish for world domination or something. I'd grown up surrounded by so much weirdness that imagining what one of my family members might have done if they'd got hold of a wishing box was enough to make me reluctant to hand it over to the public.

On the other hand, if we were careful to check that no wish was likely to result in any trouble, then what harm could it do?

"I'll test the box out later," she said. "Also, I'll keep it hidden until the main event so that we don't give away the surprise."

"Good idea. I can see Janice getting a wishing box of her own just to try to compete with us."

Janice, who owned the only other holiday inn in our part of town, was forever trying to undercut us and take away our potential customers. It annoyed her to no end that we'd put together such a big event at short notice, and I wouldn't put it past her to swipe the idea for her own at the first opportunity. It certainly wouldn't be the first time she'd done so.

Still, I was confident the wishing box would prove a hit with our guests, especially as it was the real deal. Most people would be clamouring to get in line to have the chance to make their own wishes come true.

"Yeah, I wouldn't put it past her," said Mercy. "I know for a fact that she's still mad because we snagged the best theatre group in town."

"Too right."

I walked behind the desk to the wooden door leading into the back room, which we'd converted from a supply closet to a backstage area the theatre group could use as a changing room between acts, since another door inside the room connected it to the hall where the main performance would be taking place. I entered the hall, surveying the wide stage we'd set up for the production. Rows of chairs filled the rest of the space, while tinsel hung in loops from the walls. Four days remained until the main event kicked off, and now all we needed was an audience.

I pushed some chairs into line, hearing Mercy's voice from the reception area talking to someone. A moment later, she entered the hall and beckoned me over, her usual cheer notably absent from her expression. "Carol, some guests just showed up. They look a bit… odd."

My brow furrowed. "We're at the North Pole, in a town inhabited by elves, abominable snowmen, and talking animals. What's too odd for Holiday Haven?"

"Come on," she said, looking decidedly uncomfortable. "Judge for yourself."

Wondering what had her tinsel in a tangle, I walked after her into the reception area via the back room. "We still have enough rooms for guests, don't we?"

"Of course. That's not the problem."

"Then what could possibly be odd about… them…"

I trailed off, looking in horror at my own parents, who stood in the lobby next to a collection of large suitcases. Both of them were short and blond, like me, though their thickest winter coats were bright where I tended to wear dark colours. What set us apart, though, was on their heads. Mum wore a giant red hat decorated with silver tinsel and glittering fairy lights, while Dad wore a bright-green one decked out like a Christmas tree. Even Mum's tabby cat, Charlie, wore a miniature red hat between his pointed ears.

That was the family business. Novelty hats. And boy, had I seen enough hat-related nonsense for a lifetime.

Why had they come all the way up to the North Pole for an unexpected visit this week of all possible weeks? Even by the standards of Holiday Haven, they stood out, and everyone in town would have noticed their arrival.

"Oh, hello, Carolyn." Mum's hat bounced on her forehead, its lights flashing, while I silently debated the feasibility of booking them a last-minute flight to the South Pole instead. Or going there myself.

The only person who didn't wear a hat was my sister, Bella, who sloped in behind them wearing a plain beige coat and looking about as enthused about their visit as I did. Mum's hat came close to toppling off her head as she bobbed around in excitement, taking in the stack of brochures in the reception area and the Five Years of Festive Cheer sign hanging over the door to the main hall. "Is that real snow?"

"Looks that way," Dad said. "It's great to see you, sweetheart!"

His hat burst into a loud rendition of "O Christmas Tree." Bella's expression of utter mortification matched my own, and I wished—well, if I opened that wishing box right now, I'd probably wish to turn myself into a tree ornament for the duration of their visit.

Please tell me they aren't staying until the weekend. Given their track record of unintentionally embarrassing their children, the odds of them not derailing the event were about as good as the abominable snowman developing a taste for tanning on the beach.

Why, universe? Why?

"Hey, Mum and Dad." I tried to inject enthusiasm into my tone or at least sound less horrified, but there was a reason we'd hired actual actors to take part in our play. I couldn't believe my family had come all this way without giving me warning first. Or that Bella had *let* them. She hated cold weather and was disdainful at best towards the holiday season. Imagine Scrooge as a twenty-year-old blonde and you'll get the picture. Why had she thought my parents' visit was a good idea, much less willingly come with them?

Silently apologising for being the worst daughter on the planet, I drew in a breath before lying through my teeth. "Sorry, we have an event this weekend, and all our rooms will be taken."

"I heard you," said Bella. "You do have spare rooms."

Thanks for that, Bella. Honestly, I'd have thought she'd have leapt on the chance to fly back home. What had Mum and Dad bribed her with to convince her to join them?

"We have one spare room," I corrected myself. "It's right above the reception area, in which you'll be able to hear Christmas music playing from early in the morning until night."

Bella's nose wrinkled. "One room?"

"One suite," said Mercy. "Two beds. You three will have to share a room, I'm afraid."

I hoped Bella would flat-out refuse, but no such luck. "Fine."

I tried to catch her eye, wanting to ask why on earth she'd let Mum and Dad drag her all the way up here when we both knew she'd rather be partying on a beachfront instead. Did she really miss me that much? I sincerely doubted it.

"Perfect." Mum beamed. "We'll take it. We'll be staying for a week, right?"

"I think we're leaving Monday morning," said Dad, who'd always been the slightly more organised of the pair of them despite living in the same slightly offbeat dream world as Mum did. "What was that about an event this weekend?"

I hid a grimace as Mum's familiar, Charlie, knocked a bauble off the tree and began playing with it. "Yes. Mercy and I are celebrating five years of running our holiday inn."

"Has it really been that long?" Mum asked. "To think we haven't come up to visit before now. We're long overdue."

"I've come to see you at least once per year, though." It wasn't as though I didn't call them regularly, either. It would have been nice if they'd at least mentioned their plans during our last chat before showing up here. "I don't remember when we last talked about you coming to visit."

"Nor me," said Mum. "We've been talking about coming to see you for years, haven't we? I know how busy you are, but we had a free week and Bella is off for the holidays, so... why not?"

"Why not indeed," Dad said.

I could think of plenty of reasons, but I held my tongue as Mercy handed them the keys to their room. Before they headed for the stairs, Mum went to catch her familiar, who was having the time of his life batting at the baubles on the tree.

Bella surveyed the reception area. "I expected bigger."

"We started with zero budget." I tried to keep my tone pleasant. "This place was a dilapidated shack when we first moved in. Sorry it's not a five-star hotel."

It seemed my sister still hadn't quite got over her

anger at me for taking off and leaving her to handle Mum and Dad and their hat business alone. At the time, I'd been desperate, fearing that if I didn't take the opportunity to get away, I'd be stuck at home forever. Maybe flying up to the North Pole was a bit much, but it'd worked out pretty well for us so far, as our current décor proved. Surely my sister could be the slightest bit happy for me? It was bad enough that Mum and Dad weren't interested in anything which didn't wear a ridiculous hat.

As Mum caught Charlie the cat and picked him up, I headed to the staircase to show them to their rooms and spotted Mercy taking the wishing box with her into the back room. Good job, because from the look on my sister's face, she'd already figured out what it was. I'd rather not know what she wanted to wish for, if not to get home as quickly as possible.

Why couldn't they have just called me instead?

I climbed the short staircase and led my family to their suite, and they carried their bags and suitcases inside. I didn't join in their excited chatter, unable to shake the sinking feeling that I was making a monumental mistake in letting them stay at the inn. It struck me as kind of mean to send them packing when they'd come all this way, but if they'd used magic to get here, then it wouldn't take them that long to get back home either. If I convinced them to leave, it wasn't like I was throwing them out in the cold, after all.

The wishing box came to mind. Maybe I should give it a test run myself, but if they did stay for the weekend, I'd need more luck than a wishing box could provide to get through it in one piece.

2

I left my family to settle into their room and returned to the reception area. Mercy, who was in the process of returning the baubles Charlie had knocked off the tree to their former positions, wore an expression which suggested she was almost as baffled as I was at the current turn of events. Neither of us had expected my family to show their faces here at all, let alone without any notice.

"I don't even believe this," I whispered to her. "Why are they here?"

"I hoped you could tell *me* that. Didn't you invite them?"

"I might have suggested they come and stay someday, but I didn't expect them to actually take me up on the offer." Especially at a time like this.

"Yeah, I imagine they took it as an invitation," she said. "I know what your parents are like. They were probably only half paying attention."

"You aren't wrong." Mum and Dad lived in their own

heads most of the time, under the spacious cover of their towering hats. Neither of them was exactly what you'd call grounded. Bella and I had inherited the entirety of the family's common sense. Perhaps it was nature's way of compensating for the two of them having zero attention fixed on the real world.

Mercy and I had been best friends since we were five years old, so at least I didn't have to explain my weird family to her from scratch. Still, I didn't blame her for being wary about their presence here. Especially considering our first business endeavour—an ice cream shop— had gone down in flames when Bella had decided to replace our caramel with mustard. At the time, Mum and Dad had insisted she didn't know what she was doing since she was only a teenager. As if teenagers couldn't be scheming and vindictive.

Hmm. That particular incident might account for my own wariness over the idea of letting them stay here at the inn throughout the weekend. Maybe I'd be better off convincing them to leave—through direct or indirect means. I hesitated, on the brink of going to look for the wishing box, but before I could slip into the back room, my family re-entered the reception area. At least they'd dressed appropriately for the weather in thick coats, but the sheer brightness of their hats gave Rudolph's shiny nose a run for its money, and their festive cheer would put the local carollers to shame.

"Aren't you going to give us the tour?" Mum asked. "This is such a lovely little town, isn't it?"

"We're kind of busy…" On the other hand, letting them roam around town alone might not be a wise idea. Knowing them, they'd end up borrowing a sledge and getting stuck in a snowdrift or something. It was a miracle they'd made it here without getting lost, and I suspected I had Bella to thank for that. Didn't mean she'd be willing to tail them around town and keep an eye on them, though. They didn't just go looking for trouble. They went bounding hat-first into it.

"Go on," Mercy said to me. "I'll watch the desk while you go and show them the sights."

Hmm. Maybe it was a good idea for me to keep my family busy while Mercy took over the business side of things. It wasn't like they could get into too much trouble if I kept an eye on them, right?

"Okay, I'll show you around," I said, resigned.

"Fantastic!" Mum practically skipped with excitement as she followed me out of the inn, while Dad wandered behind her, humming to himself. Bella wore her usual scowl, but she followed us without a fuss. I suspected she'd slip away as soon as my back was turned, but she wasn't the person I needed to watch. Still, if I managed to tire out my parents, I might get a spare moment to use the wishing box to convince them to fly home before the weekend. It'd take a huge weight off my mind and would also enable them to experience the highlights of Holiday Haven without risking jeopardising our event. Win-win.

Bolstered by my plan, I took the lead. The group of snow witches Mercy and I had built outside the inn proved a hit, especially when I mentioned that they hadn't melted in all the years they'd sat on either side of the doors with sculpted hats and broomsticks.

As we walked through the neighbourhood, Mum and Dad exclaimed and pointed at anything that looked remotely interesting. Which was most things, because

Holiday Haven did spectacle and style with aplomb. Clusters of carollers sang outside shop windows piled with lovingly wrapped gifts; sledges sailed past pulled by huskies and reindeer; and groups of snowmen which never melted sat on street corners. As their excitement refused to abate, I started to wonder if it would even be possible to tire them out. From their back-and-forth conversation, it sounded like they'd already amassed a dozen ideas for new hats they'd create when they got home.

Between that and the fact that Dad's hat kept breaking into song, I didn't blame Bella for backing farther and farther away from our group. I couldn't exactly pretend not to be with them, since I was their tour guide, so I took them into the confectionery shop, from which they emerged with their jaws gummed shut with delicious warm toffee. Having successfully silenced them for a few minutes, I then took them to the local café. Cheery locals wrapped in colourful scarfs and warm coats sat in huddles at tables, exchanging the latest gossip. I caught a few words about Jack Frost being missing and something about the local reindeer sanctuary, at least until their attention caught on Mum and Dad's vibrant hats. Luckily, the other customers seemed to find their hats adorable rather than cringeworthy, and we departed with takeaway cups of hot chocolate in hand.

I took a long sip, and the warmth went straight to my toes. The local hot chocolate always put me in a good mood, at least until I realised Bella hadn't come inside the café. In fact, she was nowhere to be seen.

"I think Bella wandered off," I remarked to the others.

"Oh, no," said Mum. "What if she's got herself lost?"

"I'm sure she'll be fine," I said. "She's resourceful. Anyway, she might want to explore the town by herself for a bit."

"But she doesn't know the way back to the inn, does she?" asked Dad.

"She probably remembers," I said. "Besides, everyone here is really friendly. If she asks for directions, she should easily be able to find her way back without any problems."

They both looked doubtful, but it wasn't due to lack of faith in Bella. To our parents, my little sister was the baby, and that was doubly true now I'd left home and moved up to the North Pole. I didn't really blame them for being a tad overprotective of her, but I wasn't about to go chasing after Bella when she clearly didn't want to be found.

The three of us made our way back through the snowy streets with our hot drinks in our hands and the merry atmosphere of the town staving off the chill of the ever-present snow. I'd almost begun to enjoy myself, if I ignored the fact that my parents were currently debating buying a small mountain of tinsel to make into hats. I let them indulge their curiosity at the decorations store, managing to refrain from asking how they expected to carry it all home. When they started a snowball fight on the walk back to the inn, I let them get on with that too. It wasn't like they got much in the way of real snow back in England.

As we neared the inn, however, I spotted Janice coming the other way, wearing a thick white fur coat. A scowl marred her otherwise pretty face, and she raised her eyebrows at my snowball-wielding parents.

"Who're they?" she asked. "I didn't know you were hiring circus performers for your event."

"Sure we are," I said sarcastically. "We also need some people to volunteer for target practise, if you're interested."

She had some cheek insulting my family. Granted, she'd set up her own inn in the same year as Mercy and me so it was inevitable that we'd come into competition with one another, but she could stand to be a little more pleasant. It wasn't like Mercy or I had ever done anything to her, after all. The attitude was all on her end.

At that moment, Mum aimed a snowball at Dad and missed, instead hitting Janice in the back of the head. Laughing like teenagers, they ran out of sight as Janice's face went brick-red. *Oh, boy.*

"You threw a *snowball* at me!" she spluttered, but they didn't turn back.

"See, you'll do great at target practise." I sidestepped her. "See you around."

I watched my back as I rejoined my parents, in case she decided to lob a snowball at me in retaliation, but she seemed too startled to react. Hoping Mum and Dad thought my face was flushed from the cold and not embarrassment, I continued to lead the way back to the inn.

"Oops." Mum slowed her pace. "I didn't mean to hit that girl."

"Let's hope she doesn't try to get you back for it." I veered to the right, towards the snow witches outside the inn. "Janice is known for holding grudges."

"I thought everyone was friendly here," said Dad.

"There's always one anomaly." While I might be

comparatively new to Holiday Haven, the residents had done their absolute best to make Mercy and me feel welcome. With one exception. Janice barely registered most of the time, her presence a sour note which went unheard when she wasn't swiping our ideas. Why she'd been wandering around our small corner of town, I had no idea.

I pushed the door to the inn open, wiping a sheen of snow off my sleeve. Inside, Mercy stood behind the desk with the phone in her hand, sounding slightly frazzled as she spoke to the person on the other end. Maybe she'd seen Janice herself, though I couldn't think why she'd willingly drop by for a visit.

Mum lobbed one last snowball at Dad, who bore it cheerfully before stepping into the reception area. I gave him a stern look when he moved to pick up a handful of snow from the desk, motioning to Mercy to indicate that she wouldn't appreciate them continuing their snow battle while she was on the phone.

"I hope Bella finds her way back," Mum said to me, thankfully getting the message.

"She will," I said. "I'll wait for her down here. You go and change before you catch a cold."

Mum and Dad went to their room to change out of their snow-covered clothes, while I hovered in the entryway. I hoped my sister *didn't* get lost, but I couldn't picture her staying outside in the snow for long. I also hoped she didn't run into Janice, come to that. If the two of them came to blows, I wasn't entirely sure who'd come off worse.

Mercy hung up the phone. "Marcus is being so *demanding*. You'd think we were hiring him to act in the

West End, not a low-budget theatre production for a few tourists. How'd the tour go, anyway?"

"Fine, until Bella ran off. I'm sure she'll be able to find her way back, but she's prone to being a little... unfriendly. Let's just say she wouldn't fit in here at Holiday Haven."

"I noticed," she said dryly.

"I saw Janice outside too. Mum accidentally hit her with a snowball."

"Oh, great. Bet she loved that."

"If someone sends us reindeer dung in the mail, we'll know who's responsible," I said. "I wondered if she dropped by here."

"I didn't see her, but she was probably sneaking a look through the window. I bet she's kicking herself for not thinking of hiring out her inn to put on a theatrical production."

"She's scoping out the competition, I guess," I added, thinking of the nasty look on her face when she'd seen my parents. At the memory, an odd defensiveness took hold of me. I might be embarrassed on my family's behalf on a regular basis, but that didn't mean I appreciated it when people like Janice made insulting comments about them.

Mercy rolled her eyes. "I wouldn't mind foisting Marcus on her, I wouldn't lie. But his theatre group is the best in town, even if they act like divas sometimes."

"What's his problem, then?" I asked.

"The costumes haven't arrived yet. Which would be because I only just ordered them. I forked out for expedited shipping, so they ought to show up by tomorrow morning at the latest, with plenty of time before the dress rehearsal."

"Exactly," I said. "The dress rehearsal, though... I can't entertain my family while supervising the theatre group at the same time."

"I know. I wish I could guarantee it'll all go without a hitch. It'd be a huge weight off my mind."

"Would the wishing box be able to do that? That's one way to give it a test run. I can wish for a guarantee that the event goes as planned."

That would be much better than asking my parents to leave. Aside from Bella's disappearance, we hadn't had a bad time on our tour of Holiday Haven, and if it was possible for us to enjoy the event despite our unexpected guests, then I'd do my best to make that a reality.

"Oh, good idea," she said. "I did look up the instructions for using the box, and it sounds like it ought to work as long as you're specific with what you wish for. If you wish for good luck, it's too vague, but if you mention the event in your wish, it ought to work out just fine."

"I like the way you think. Where'd you put the box?"

"Should still be in the back room."

I pushed open the door at the back of the reception area, scanning the small space within. The coat rack and shelves we'd put in there for the theatre group remained in place, but there was no sign of the wishing box anywhere in the room.

"Where'd you leave it?" I crouched down and peered under the shoe rack then behind the table.

Mercy's voice came drifting through the door. "On the table. Why?"

"It's not here." I rose to my feet and searched every inch of the room, dread rising inside me when I still found no sign of the box. I then pushed open the door connecting the room to the main hall, finding it empty aside from the rows of chairs lined in front of the stage. The gleaming box would have stood out by a mile, but nobody but Mercy would have moved it. Right?

"Has anyone else been in here?" I re-entered the back room, trying to keep the panic out of my voice.

"Not that I'm aware of." She joined me, her eyes widening with concern. "It can't be gone. Nobody has been in here except me."

Mercy and I did another thorough examination of the room before moving to search the hall. At the back, a rarely used emergency exit drew my attention like a neon sign. "You don't think anyone sneaked in through the hall while you were on the phone and stole it? When was the last time you came in here?"

Her eyes rounded. "Before you left the inn."

How many people had even known we had the wishing box, much less had been able to access the back room without Mercy spotting them? Mum and Dad might not have seen the box earlier, but Bella had, and of the three, she was the person most likely to want to take it for herself. Even if she didn't actually want to wish for anything, she might have just wanted to annoy me. If she'd intended to use it to wish herself away from here, I almost didn't blame her, but she was the one who'd offered to accompany my parents in the first place. Besides, the box was ours.

Out of any other ideas, I made for the stairs up to my parents' suite and nearly collided with Bella entering through the front door.

"Oh, good, you found your way back," I said.

She grunted and walked upstairs ahead of me, trailing

snowy footprints in her wake. "You managed to get Mum and Dad back in one piece, then?"

"More or less. They did buy half the tinsel from the decorations shop." I paused for an instant then followed her upstairs. "Also, have you seen a box? We're missing one."

She didn't turn back. "What kind of box?"

"A box covered in gemstones. It's disappeared from the back room. You saw it when you first showed up here, right? Mercy had it."

"I don't remember a box."

I didn't believe she'd really forgotten, but I'd rather avoid kicking off a pointless argument if it turned out she wasn't responsible for its disappearance. I caught her up at the top of the stairs where the door led to the suite she and my parents shared. One peek through the door showed me an entire menagerie of hats had already taken over the room.

"Carolyn!" said Mum. "Want to come and try on these hats? We could use a model."

Oh, boy. "No, thanks."

If the box had ended up in their room by mistake, there was no way I'd be able to track it down hidden in that mess. It probably wasn't worth worrying too much if Bella had 'borrowed' it, but it'd vanished right when I needed it most.

I returned to the reception area, my mood dimming. Who'd been near the inn in the last few hours? Janice's face swam to the forefront of my mind. She hadn't sneaked in here and taken the box, had she? It wasn't like I'd be able to prove it if she had, but it was just the sort of thing she'd do.

Regardless of who'd taken it, without the box, I couldn't send my parents back home before the weekend. They'd be staying here for the duration… and now there was no guarantee the event would go ahead without a hitch.

I'd just have to deal with all the potential problems the regular way, then. Without magic.

3

I left my parents and Bella upstairs in their room while Mercy and I made yet another attempt to find our missing wishing box. By now, we'd combed the entire downstairs floor and a fair bit of the upstairs too. Since neither of us had removed it from the back room, someone else must have done so. Even a magic box couldn't disappear into thin air, as far as I knew.

"Are you positive you didn't see anyone go into that room?" I asked Mercy.

"I can't honestly say I paid attention. Not when I was dealing with Marcus's complaints on the phone, anyway."

"It's okay," I reassured her. "It's not your fault. I wasn't even around most of the day. Maybe we shouldn't have opened the package as soon as it showed up."

"Well, it's not like the wishing box was absolutely essential for the event to go ahead as planned. Nobody knew about it except for the two of us."

"Exactly. We'll keep an eye out for it and carry on as normal."

Though I might well need both of my eyes to keep my family under close watch, to be honest. Even leaving them alone in their room wouldn't prevent them from plotting mischief, and I could never entirely forget the mayhem they'd got up to when Bella and I were kids. Memories of my teachers' bewilderment and my peers' relentless mocking during their rare visits to the witch academy when I was a student were burned into my brain, and even back then, I'd understood that they were weird even by the magical world's standards. Years on, the urge to hide their shenanigans from everyone else was ingrained, but I did my best to push it out of mind as Mercy and I resumed our preparations for the event.

The rest of the afternoon passed quickly until my family came back downstairs that evening for dinner. We had a simple menu for the inn's small restaurant, but most guests preferred to eat in and didn't mind the lack of selection. Bella, however, looked less than impressed as she sat down with our parents at a cosy table in a corner.

"What kind of entertainment do you have at night?" She picked up a menu and brushed off some glittery strands from the tinsel hanging overhead.

"Entertainment?" I echoed.

"Yes, you know," she said. "Singing, dancing, that kind of thing?"

"We don't have entertainment every night." The local carollers often came to visit, but they had a limited repertoire of songs. "We have music, but only festive-themed songs."

"Oh, great."

I bit back the urge to ask what she'd expected from a town called Holiday Haven and said, "If you're staying for the weekend's event, there's a full theatrical production on Saturday and a lot more entertainment planned. Usually, we don't have the audience for it."

The theatre company's dress rehearsal was set for noon tomorrow, and my nerves spiked at the prospect of going through with it with my family still here. Bella's expression remained unimpressed throughout the evening, though it didn't help that Mum and Dad had also discovered the town's most popular brand of eggnog, and consequently, were rowdier than ever at dinner. Thankfully, they managed to refrain from doing anything too outrageous other than asking the other guests for their opinions on festive hats. Pretty harmless, all things considered.

Soon enough, they tottered off to bed, pursued by Charlie. I had to stop the cat from swiping some of the table decorations on the way out, and when I found Bella tailing behind, I waylaid her before she could catch up to our parents. "Why did you come here?"

"Why'd you think?" she said. "To stop them from getting into trouble."

"You didn't have to. I know you hate the Christmas holidays, and we're kind of short on any other theme here."

She gave a shrug. "So? Doesn't mean I thought it was a good idea for them to go off to the North Pole alone. Knowing them, they'd have ended up at the South Pole instead."

"Couldn't you have talked them out of it?"

"I haven't tried to talk them out of anything since that time when I was six and they wanted to send me to school wearing that hat shaped like a traffic light."

I hadn't known she remembered those occasions as vividly as I did. We both knew that there was no stopping either of our parents when they were on a mission, but she didn't have to tag along with them. Knowing how much she hated snow, I felt a smidgeon of sympathy towards her for how stuck she must have felt.

"Yeah, it's not great timing," I admitted. "We're preparing for a major event, as I told you. It ought to be fine, but we're run off our feet this week."

"Found that box of yours yet?" she asked.

"No. I'm sure it'll turn up. It's not absolutely necessary anyway."

I spoke more to reassure myself than anything, though Bella had never struck me as particularly interested in whether I succeeded or failed. Mustard incident aside, she hadn't outright interfered with any of our plans for a long while. She ought to be more mature now, surely.

The long afternoon of entertaining the family had tired me out, so I went to bed not long after the other guests did. Mercy and I slept in adjacent rooms on the very top floor of the inn, under the sloping roofs. Normally, the pleasant views of the moonlit town from the windows lulled me to sleep in no time, but tonight, my mind remained restless, and every glance out the window made me fervently hope that Mum and Dad didn't get any wild ideas of going for a nocturnal wander in the snow. When I finally drifted off, I ended up in a disturbing dream about being buried up to my neck in a snowdrift. No matter how hard I tried, the heavy snow weighed on me like a blanket, pinning down my limbs.

A violent shiver woke me, and I opened my eyes to find bright snowflakes drifting down from the ceiling. It hadn't all been a dream after all. A layer of pure white covered my bed like a second duvet, soaking through the sheets to my pyjamas.

"What the—?" I looked up at the ceiling, half-expecting to see the roof had opened to the elements. Instead, it seemed to be snowing *inside* the room, large flakes drifting down and covering everything from the en suite bathroom to the carpets. There was snow in the shower. Snow on my bookshelves. Snow in my shoes.

"Mercy?" I called out.

No reply came. She could sleep through an earthquake, but she'd never made it snow in her sleep before. While I was perfectly happy to wander for hours in the snow, wrapped up in warm layers, I'd prefer not to have it in my bed. I would not be amused if I ended up catching a cold before the weekend, for that matter.

Luck was with me and the snow hadn't got into my wardrobe, so after I'd salvaged some clothes from the snow-free part of my room and dried myself off before getting dressed in warm layers, I went downstairs to check up on my family. Mercy still hadn't stirred, but piles of snow filled the corridor too. Flakes drifted down from the ceiling all the way downstairs to the lowest floor.

I descended, careful not to slip on the snow-slick carpet, and Bella poked her head out of my family's suite with snowflakes tangled in her blond hair and a glower on her face. "Is this your idea of a joke?"

"No," I said. "Is the snow inside your room too?"

"What do you think?" She squelched backwards and yanked open the door, revealing a room full of snow-covered hats. Mum sat on the bed, a disconcerting smile on her face.

"Isn't it nice?" said Mum. "We don't get this kind of snow at home."

"Nice!" Bella said. "I have snow in my suitcase and on all my clothes."

"You can dry them easily," said Dad, who looked as delighted as Mum did. "It's harmless."

"It's *not* harmless," Bella fumed.

Charlie meowed piteously, half-buried in a pile of snow. Sensing a major family argument was imminent, I backed away. The snowflakes, meanwhile, kept falling from the ceiling, while footsteps came from above, suggesting the other guests were stirring too.

"I need to figure out how to stop this spell," I told my family. "I'll come back."

I headed back upstairs, hearing Bella snapping at Mum and Dad in the background. Hoping Mercy had a solution, I returned to the top floor, where I found her standing blearily in the doorway to her room, shaking snow off her pyjama sleeves. "What's going on?"

"I wish I knew," I said. "The whole inn has been hit by some kind of blizzard spell. It won't stop."

"Seriously? I wondered if I accidentally used my magic in my sleep, but I've never made it snow over this big an area before."

"It's in every single room. Bella is furious. Mum and Dad are thrilled, of course, but I can't figure out how to stop it. Please tell me you have some idea."

She rubbed her eyes. "Not if we don't know where it's coming from. I'll be down in a second."

"Sure," I said. "Fair warning, I think the other guests are awake."

Two of them had planned to fly back home that day, so

I gave them a discount on their final bills as an apology for the inconvenience as they checked out. I had a heart-stopping moment where I thought the snow had got inside the computer, but it turned on once I dried it off. Our phone had somehow survived, too, but all our chairs were soaked through, and so were the carpets. Nowhere had been spared. The real casualty was my new handmade banner, which now lay in a soggy, crumpled mess in the corner. Mourning my hard work, I rolled it up and stashed it underneath the desk.

Not long after we'd seen off the departing guests, Mum and Dad walked in, wearing identical reindeer hats dusted with powder-white snow.

"Isn't this fun?" Mum asked. "I don't know what Bella is complaining about."

"It could be worse," I allowed. "I don't suppose either of you two knows how to stop a magically conjured snowstorm? Neither of us have managed to figure it out, and Mercy *has* winter-themed magic of her own."

"I'll see what I can think of," said Mum. "Where's breakfast?"

"In there." I pointed to the door leading into the small restaurant, which was also buried in snow. Not that it bothered either of my parents. They were happy enough eating cornflakes with snow instead of milk while I cleared piles of snow off the coffee machine. The only person more miserable than Bella was Charlie the cat. When he couldn't find a snow-free spot to sit in, he ran for the door outside with a piteous wail.

"He won't find a dry place to hide out there," I said. "It never stops snowing here."

"This has Janice written all over it," Mercy said

through chattering teeth. "Bet she thought it was hilarious."

"You think it's revenge for the snowball incident?" Maybe. I didn't know anyone else who harboured such a grudge against us that they'd make it snow inside our guests' rooms. "I can't tell whether the spell was cast inside the building or not."

"I'd guess not, unless she wanted to risk getting caught breaking and entering," Mercy said. "The spell can't keep it snowing forever, though. Especially if she isn't in the area."

If we'd had the wishing box, we might have been able to reverse the spell easily enough, but we didn't. Typical. "I hope you're right."

Her expression brightened. "On the plus side, at least it fits the theme. It's not like it's raining frogs or something."

At that moment, Bella wandered into the reception area, her blond hair tucked into her furry hood. "I can't believe you live at the North Pole and you don't know how to stop it snowing."

"I don't normally *want* to stop it snowing," I informed her.

She rolled her eyes. "You seriously like this cold wet stuff?"

"Yes. Granted, I'd rather it wasn't in my room, but it usually snows *outside.* Not indoors."

"Well, I want it gone. What are you doing about it?"

"Trying to figure out where it came from. I think it's the type of spell which will run its course within a few hours unless we find the culprit and get them to stop it, and we don't know who that is."

Nor did we have any proof of Janice's involvement.

The snow was a minor nuisance, really, not something worth involving the police over. Unless she'd been the one who'd taken the wishing box, too, of course.

"Someone threw a snowstorm at you on purpose?" asked Bella.

"It's not likely to be an accident. Not if the spell was cast in the middle of the night while we were sleeping, anyway."

I wasn't about to confront Janice in person until we'd exhausted all our options for getting rid of our impromptu snowstorm, and I definitely wouldn't stoop to begging her to reverse the spell. Even if she *was* the culprit, she had better things to do than torment us all day, surely.

Bella shook her head and walked away, leaving me and Mercy alone in the reception area.

"My guess is that someone cast the spell over the building and then walked off," said Mercy. "It ought to have a time limit on it… but it isn't showing any signs of stopping yet."

"What if it's still snowing when we hold the dress rehearsal?" I could only imagine what the theatre group would have to say to that. Picturing Marcus's face if he found snow in the dressing room would have been amusing under any other circumstances, but it'd escalate from a minor inconvenience to a major one if it derailed our rehearsal.

"The snow works as a backdrop for the show," said Mercy. "We'll just have to tell them not to start throwing snowballs at one another when they're supposed to be rehearsing."

"And the costumes aren't here yet either," I added. "Maybe we can reschedule."

Though given that it was already Wednesday, moving the rehearsal to a later date would be cutting it close to the start of the event.

"I'll see if it stops in a couple of hours," she said. "What're your parents doing today, do you know?"

"Haven't a clue." For all I knew, they'd be happy to stay in their room and build snowmen, but they'd get bored eventually. Our tour yesterday had gone fine, so there were worse things to do than find ways for them to entertain themselves outside. The rather soggy collection of brochures near the desk advertised the various forms of entertainment on offer, from tours of the present-making factories to visits to the reindeer sanctuary.

"You don't think one of them cast the spell, did they?" Mercy whispered. "Not that I want to accuse your family or anything, but they seem to be having fun with it."

I glanced over at Mum and Dad, who'd started a snowball fight in the doorway of the restaurant. "Probably not, but maybe they can help me figure out how to stop it. Once we've exhausted all the other options, anyway."

For now, I needed to get them out of here before the theatre group showed up—and before Bella lost her temper altogether.

4

After selecting a few brochures to look at, my parents followed me out of the inn, still lobbing snowballs at one another. My goal was to get them exhausted enough not to cause trouble later on, but they had more energy than toddlers hyped up on sugar and an unending sense of adventure. If anything, I was the one who needed to lie down after the first hour of following them around the snow-laden streets.

And I was still none the wiser as to where the snow spell had come from, nor where the wishing box had disappeared to. In fairness, it was kind of impossible to get a word in edgeways to ask my parents any questions while they kept running around throwing snowballs and trying to knock one another's hats off.

Bella, meanwhile, grew more and more visibly annoyed until a snowball misfired and hit her in the back of the head. At once, she wheeled on both of our parents with a snarl of annoyance. "Can you cut that out?"

Both my parents looked startled to hear her yell at them, and they exchanged concerned glances.

"Sorry," said Mum. "Won't do it again."

They stopped throwing snowballs, at least, but they retained their air of eagerness and excitement as we continued on. At least they'd slowed down enough for me to keep pace with them without risking taking a snowball to the face, so I fell into step with them.

"I don't suppose either of you has seen a box?" I asked.

"What kind of box, sweetheart?" asked Mum.

"About the size of my palm and decorated with jewels. It disappeared at some point yesterday from the back room of the inn."

"Oh, that one?" she said. "It's a wishing box, isn't it?"

"Wait, you saw it?" I asked, disarmed.

"Yes, it was on the desk, wasn't it?"

"It was." Before Mercy had taken it into the back room, anyway. I hadn't known they'd been paying attention at the time. "It went missing at some point yesterday. If it hadn't, we could have used it to get the snow to stop."

"Oh, I'm sure you won't need to resort to that. It'll stop by itself, I imagine."

I hoped so, but that wouldn't make the box come back. I opened my mouth to say so, then I noticed Bella had walked far ahead of our group, perhaps to avoid getting hit by another snowball. When Dad crept up behind her, holding a handful of snow, I shook my head in warning. Getting the message, he took aim at Mum's hat instead.

After we'd walked for a while, my phone buzzed with a message from Mercy back at the inn. It sounded like the costumes for the theatre group had finally shown up.

"Our delivery for the weekend's event showed up," I

told my parents. "I should check on that. You two will be okay, won't you?"

"Don't worry," said Mum. "We can take care of ourselves."

I didn't particularly want to leave them to wander around the town while they were in such an excitable mood, but as long as they refrained from hitting anyone else with a wayward snowball, they ought to be fine. Besides, it'd be best for them to stay away from our costume arrival in case they started suggesting ways to improve everything with absurd hats. It was safe to say that Marcus from the theatre group would not be in favour of that idea.

"Okay, but let me know if you need me," I said. "I don't want you catching colds either, considering you both got drenched in snow earlier."

"There's no need to worry about us," Mum insisted.

"Exactly," said Dad. "We'll be just fine."

Bella shot me a raised eyebrow, but she refrained from making one of her usual comments about me being the boring one in the family. Since I was an older sibling, I'd realised before Bella had that Mum and Dad just weren't great at conventional parenting, so I'd taken on the role almost unconsciously. Having creative parents had its perks, but not when it came to remembering appointments or getting us to school on time. It'd taught me to be self-reliant, if nothing else, a trait which had helped when Mercy and I had started our business from scratch. Bella, though, harboured a little more resentment than I did.

I waved my family off and then walked back to the inn, where a group of post owls flew above my head in a flurry of tawny feathers. At least the costume delivery had shown up on time, proving Marcus's complaints had been for nothing. He'd been irritatingly controlling throughout every aspect of the experience, but since neither Mercy nor I had any acting experience to speak of, we'd known from the moment we'd started writing the script that we'd have to hire professionals. We'd been lucky Marcus had said yes, and the theatre group had given a much-needed boost to our ticket sales. Normally, I'd be looking forward to seeing it all come together, but if Marcus showed up before the snow stopped, he'd throw a fit. Or possibly a snowball.

Mercy met me at the door to the inn. "Want the good news or the bad news?"

"What good news?" I asked.

"The snow stopped." She gestured at the newly sparkling clean reception area. "Looks like the spell wore out by itself."

"Oh, good," I said, relief sweeping over me. "I guess the spell had a time limit on it after all."

"Yeah, I figured it would. It's the sort of spell that can't go on forever, especially if the caster didn't stick around."

Considering I hadn't seen Janice outside, I guessed she'd cast her spell and wandered off, content with leaving some temporary mayhem behind. "Okay… what's the bad news?"

Marcus's booming voice came from the back room. "Where to start?"

Oh, boy. I caught Mercy's eye and mouthed, *He's here early?*

Mercy widened her eyes in response, and I found myself thanking whatever lucky stars had intervened for stopping the snow before he'd got here. As the head of the theatre group, Marcus was directing the play, though he'd also taken on the part of one of Santa's reindeer. We did have real reindeer in town, but neither of us wanted to deal with the mess, so it was much easier to use people in costumes instead.

I'd remained sceptical about Marcus agreeing to wear a pair of antlers, but he took the part as seriously as any other and managed to parade around directing the other actors without anyone laughing. Admittedly, that might change when he put on the actual costume.

"There's a slight issue," Mercy said, indicating the pile of cardboard boxes stacked next to the counter. "The costumes showed up, and... well."

Marcus walked out of the back room, wearing a brown costume which covered him from head to toe. The slight problem was that instead of antlers, a giant pair of rabbit ears protruded from the top of his head. Complete with his grumpy expression, it made a real picture, and I suppressed the urge to break into giggles.

"This is an Easter Bunny costume," he informed me. "What is the meaning of this?"

"You think I know?" I looked at Mercy, who was also stifling a laugh behind her hand. "I thought we ordered them from a reputable online shop. Don't tell me all the other costumes are the same too."

"Okay, I won't tell you." Mercy hid her laugh with a cough. "All of them are identical, I'm afraid."

Sure enough, two other members of the theatre group walked out of the back room, also dressed as rabbits. As amusing as they looked, our reindeer would either have to undergo a quick transformation into rabbits in the script or we'd need to find an alternative costume source within the next few days.

"Maybe we can tweak the script a little so that Santa's sleigh is pulled by bunnies instead of reindeer," said Mercy. "It's not the worst idea."

"Would we have to sing 'Rudolph the Red-Nosed Bunny'?" asked one of the actors.

"That doesn't work at all!" said Marcus, his face as red as Rudolph's nose. "This is ridiculous. I was promised a professional production."

"You're trained actors," I said. "Surely you can improvise. Besides, we still have time to sort out this little mishap."

"I don't mind playing a rabbit," said Daryl, another member of the group, whose tall frame made his rabbit ears droop under the doorway. "It'll make us more memorable. Every play has reindeer in it."

"That is entirely the point!" Marcus yelled at him, making him flinch. "I want this situation rectified at once."

The door opened with a sweep of cold air, and several people entered the reception area behind me. It seemed the rest of the theatre group had come to see the costumes, and when they set eyes on their leader, they burst into uncontrollable laughter.

I ducked out of the line of fire as Marcus's face flushed with anger, and Mercy took the initiative and darted behind the desk to boot up the computer. While Marcus shouted semi-coherently at his fellow actors, Mercy looked up the confirmation email from the online shop and showed it to me. "Look, it's definitely a set of reindeer costumes I ordered."

I peered at the screen. The same order showed up on the receipt, too, which suggested there'd been a mistake on the shop's end.

"Look." I beckoned Marcus over to the desk. "The order was the right one. There must have been a mix-up."

"Evidently, someone made a mistake," Marcus said. "You'll have to send a complaint to the shop. And if they don't send replacements at once, we will no longer be acting in your play."

He marched into the back room, presumably to change into his regular clothes again. The other actors had mostly stopped laughing by now, hovering guiltily in front of the desk as he slammed the door behind him.

"We'll call the shop on the phone and ask if they can send some replacements," I suggested. "I'll pay expedited shipping if I have to. I don't mind."

"All right," Mercy said. "I don't think there's anything wrong with Santa's sleigh being pulled by giant rabbits, personally."

If Marcus pulled out of the show, though, he'd take half the cast along with him if not all of them. They all hero-worshiped him despite his temper, which made it paramount that we find a way to deal with our unfortunate Easter Bunny situation as soon as possible.

While Mercy made the call, I went to the hall in order to check on the remaining damage from our impromptu snowstorm. Really, we were lucky the snow hadn't hit the costumes, because we'd have had a tough job returning them to the shop if they were soaked through. Thanking the universe for small mercies, I beckoned the rest of the theatre group into the hall and crossed my fingers behind my back that nobody would accidentally sit on any of the damp seats.

Returning to the reception area, I dug out the banner which had fallen off the wall earlier and found it'd more or less dried out. The damage wasn't as bad as I'd feared, since the snow had smudged the words a little but hadn't ruined my glow-in-the-dark spell. I retrieved the stepladder and set about hanging the banner above the door in its former position while I waited for Mercy to finish the call so we could kick off the rehearsal.

On the phone, Mercy's tone grew more and more agitated. "No, it's really true. They're definitely rabbit costumes. Do you want me to take a photo and send it to you?"

More talking came from the other end. Then she said, "Yes, I know, but we can't do our production with rabbits and not reindeer. I wish we could, but I'm going to have to return them… yes, I'll use the form. Thanks. Bye."

She hung up, shaking her head.

"No luck?" I asked.

Mercy pursed her lips. "They're insisting they were reindeer costumes when they put the boxes in the post. So unless they transformed into rabbits halfway through their journey here, something's awry."

"Can they prove it? Because that sounds like an excuse to me."

"I know. We can't go ahead like this, though, not as long as Marcus…" She trailed off, gesturing at the closed door to the back room.

"We can still do the rehearsal, though. Are you going to order replacements?"

"I have to use their online form." She returned to the

computer. "I'll send it through, and then we'll get on with the dress rehearsal."

"Preferably before my parents come back here," I added. "They were chasing around having snowball fights like little kids."

"Oh, fun. At least they're enjoying their holiday."

"Gotta make the most of those silver linings." I glanced in the direction of the hall when I heard Marcus's raised voice inside. Assuming he'd vacated the back room, I went in and retrieved the discarded rabbit costumes to put back into the boxes.

As I was packing them up again, Mercy hit the computer keyboard with her hand. "Come on, that's not fair."

I closed the lid of the box. "You okay?"

"The form won't go through," she said. "I keep getting an error message."

"Typical. Maybe try again later."

"Right." She pushed away from the computer, her forehead scrunching up. "I really don't see what the big deal is about rabbits and not reindeer pulling Santa's sleigh, to tell you the truth."

"If only Marcus was easier to convince. Maybe he'll cheer up if the dress rehearsal goes well."

5

Thankfully, the rehearsal itself didn't go too badly. If you discounted the fact that nobody was in costume, anyway, but the theatre group were good enough actors that they hid their annoyance at the situation under a veneer of festive cheer which almost made me forget the trial of a day I'd had so far. Even if my concern for my parents returned when they still hadn't come back from their trip by the time the rehearsal came to an end. Bella hadn't either, though she probably assumed the inn was still covered in snow and wanted to avoid it until we'd cleared up her room.

I couldn't say I blamed her, since I was still randomly finding piles of snow melting in corners and on top of cabinets. Marcus pointedly ignored Mercy and me on his way out of the inn after the rehearsal had finished, but if anything, it was an improvement on being glowered at. After most of the theatre group had departed, Mercy began another attempt to order the right costumes.

Behind me, the door to the back room jostled as

the stragglers from the theatre group prepared to leave. I spotted Daryl among them, eyeing Mercy hopefully, but she didn't notice him. That was nothing new. Everyone knew of his raging crush on my co-worker except for Mercy herself. When he was the last remaining person in the room, I went to rescue him.

"Hey," I said. "Something I can help you with? Mercy is dealing with the costume situation if you want to talk to her."

"Um…" He glanced at her, then back at me. "I heard you were ordering a wishing box."

"How did you know that?" That, I hadn't expected. "Did Mercy tell you?"

"Oh, am I not supposed to know?" Alarm flickered across his features. "I'm sorry. I thought it was okay."

"It is." Or rather, it would have been if the box hadn't gone *missing.* On top of the costume mix-up, it felt like someone was doing their level best to stop the show going ahead as planned. "I mean, we were trying to keep it quiet until the big event. Why?"

"Because I, uh, wanted to borrow it."

Given the flush on his face, I could hazard a guess as to what purpose he wanted to use it for. Dropping my voice, I said, "If you want Mercy to ask you out, then you're better off making a move yourself instead of relying on a box."

He shuffled from one foot to the other, his face turning a deep maroon. "I wasn't… I mean. I thought the box might give me the courage to go ahead with it. I don't even know if she returns my feelings, though."

"Not sure that's something a wishing box can control.

Besides, I'm not an expert, but I think she'd prefer it if you took the initiative."

If Mercy *didn't* return his affections, I wasn't sure even a wishing box would be able to help him. Not that it mattered now the box had vanished before we ever got the chance to test its limits.

"Oh," he said. "Okay, that's fine. I actually had a few questions about how the box might work. What kind of wishes are most likely to work?"

"We haven't tested it yet." How'd he had time to assemble a list of questions? Who'd told him we'd planned on ordering the wishing box, for that matter? Even I hadn't known until Mercy had opened the package.

"Okay," he said. "Never mind."

I opened my mouth to ask if he'd seen the box, but Marcus's voice drifted in from the reception area again, and I reluctantly suppressed my questions. I'd assumed the rest of the group had left, but apparently their melodramatic leader had decided to stick around to hassle Mercy about the costumes again.

All the same, I couldn't help wondering if Daryl wasn't being entirely honest with me. Would he have gone as far as to take the wishing box behind our backs in order to gather the courage to ask Mercy out? Or had his questions been innocent and he hadn't a clue it was missing? He shouldn't have even known we had it, which seemed a major red flag in my book.

I walked out of the back room to find Marcus glowering at Mercy over the counter. "I hope you've sorted out that costume order. I won't be pleased if it turns out we've wasted our time on this play."

"I'm trying to get the online form to go through," Mercy said. "I'll let you know when it does."

"We'll have it sorted before the weekend," I said with more certainty than I really felt. "It's not a huge deal, besides. Could be a lot worse."

"I shudder to think what your idea of 'worse' might be," he said.

I could think of a dozen even less appropriate costumes which might have shown up instead. At least rabbits were vaguely relevant. They just needed to wear some tinsel, and they'd be good to go. The audience certainly wouldn't be any the wiser, anyway. But voicing that thought aloud wouldn't do any good, so I stepped aside to let the rest of the group walk past.

"We'll let you know if we have any updates," Mercy told them.

"I should hope you do." Marcus gave Daryl a glare as the other actor shuffled out from the dressing room before leading the group out of the inn. When they'd gone, Mercy and I exchanged relieved glances.

"I really like it when people are cooperative." I gave an eye roll. "Makes things much easier."

Mercy moved back to the computer. "I'll have to keep trying to submit that form, but I don't see why they can't handle it over the phone rather than making me use their glitchy computer system."

"You'd think they'd be willing to help out a customer," I said.

"They were downright rude to me on the phone earlier. Not at all what I expected. We could just eat the costs and order the costumes from somewhere else, but there aren't a ton of places with expedited shipping to the North Pole."

"Yeah, that's the downside to living in a remote location. Maybe they shipped the reindeer costumes to the wrong address and we got someone else's order instead?"

"Who else in town ordered a dozen rabbit costumes?"

"Hopefully not my parents," I said. "Maybe we can talk to the others in the theatre group and get them to outvote Marcus on the rabbit costumes. It's not like it's going to ruin the whole show if they have floppy rabbit ears and not antlers."

"You know how seriously he takes everything, though. And he's already mad at me because he didn't know the costume was the wrong one before he put it on."

"I can think of worse mistakes than him ending up as a rabbit. Imagine if we'd got twelve sexy nurse costumes instead."

"He'd have shouted loudly enough to be heard from Santa's palace." Mercy giggled. "I shouldn't laugh. You're right. That's way worse."

"Come on, imagine his face." I grinned. "I should have offered him one of my parents' hats to hide the rabbit ears. There's a yellow flowery one which would go really well with his hair…"

Mercy hiccoughed with laughter. "Carol, I'm not going to be able to look at his face now without imagining that."

"Good. Honestly, though, he's just being picky. The others might not agree with him. I can see Daryl going for the rabbit script rewrite, for one."

"Daryl?" she asked.

I debated inwardly for a moment, then said, "Yeah. I spoke to him a minute ago, and he asked a couple of questions about the wishing box. It sounded like he wanted to know how it worked."

She blinked. "Why would he want to use it?"

"I don't know," I lied. If she didn't know about his crush on her, then I'd rather not be the one to ruin the surprise. Besides, maybe he was innocent after all and I was just being paranoid.

After all, there were other, more likely, candidates who might have stolen the box.

With the rehearsal done, sorting out the event's catering was next on the list. Since neither of us were expert chefs, we'd asked our usual staff to work on a special menu for the weekend. The slight problem, as we found out when the staff showed up mid-afternoon, was that it'd snowed all over the kitchen, and now half the ingredients were unusable.

"Oh, no," said Mercy. "I didn't even think of that."

The head chef, a local elf called Angus, was usually friendly faced, but he wasn't smiling at the moment. "Why is everything in the kitchen all wet?"

"An accident," I said. "Someone conjured up a snowstorm inside the inn, and it hit every single room, including the kitchens."

"Well, all the ingredients we'd saved for the weekend's events are ruined," said Angus. "I hope the guests don't mind adjustments to our menu for dinner."

"We'd be happy to order fresh ingredients for the weekend," Mercy said. "Sorry for the inconvenience."

He frowned at her. "Are you sure you didn't conjure up the snowstorm yourself?"

"Of course not," Mercy said. "I have better control over my magic than that."

"Well, I hope it doesn't happen again." The chef retreated into the kitchen, grumbling to himself.

"*I* hope we have room in our budgets for new ingredients," I murmured to Mercy. "Money's getting tight."

"That on top of replacing the costumes, I know," Mercy said in an undertone. "We'll just have to try extra hard to sell all our tickets."

"And make sure it doesn't happen again," I added. "Janice ought to pay for the ingredients, really, except we have no proof she's the one who actually conjured the snowstorm."

It didn't help my concerns that my parents and sister still hadn't come back from their excursion, so they must have gone somewhere in town for lunch. Perhaps they'd started another epic snowball fight and lost track of time, but I wished one of them would take some responsibility. I didn't have time to chase them around all day, especially now.

While we waited for their return, Mercy and I made yet more failed attempts to navigate the costume shop's online form.

"Maybe I should call the local costume shop instead," I said, resigned. "Might as well have a backup plan. I don't see why we can't order a set of cheap reindeer antlers to attach to the rabbit costumes and consider it done."

She arched a brow. "Think Marcus would find that acceptable?"

I groaned. "This wouldn't be a problem if he didn't mind being a rabbit. Anyway, those costumes would be fine if we just removed the bunny ears and replaced them with antlers."

"If the audience doesn't look too closely."

"They're not expecting perfection, are they? Marcus's team might be the best of the local groups, but they have as low a budget as we do. We can't pull handfuls of money out of thin air."

"Tell me about it." Mercy grabbed a notepad. "Okay, I'm going to make a list of all the ingredients we need. Can you handle the costume shop?"

"Sure."

While Mercy went to talk to the kitchen staff, I made a call to Holiday Haven's main costume shop.

"Hello?" said a male voice on the other end.

"Hey, this is Carol, from the holiday inn. I wondered if we could place an order for a dozen reindeer costumes, since we're putting on an event this weekend?"

"Ah, Carol and Mercy, right? I wish I could help you, but I'm afraid we already sold all our reindeer costumes we had in stock."

"All of them?" I said disbelievingly. "Every single costume?"

"Every reindeer costume. There's a group next week who are putting on a production of *Rudolph the Red-Nosed Reindeer*, and they needed them all."

"Which group?" I asked. "It can't be Marcus's group… they're with us."

"Ah, it's an amateur group which is brand new. Hired by… what's her name again? Janice?"

"Janice." *How typical.* It had to have been a deliberate move on her part. I didn't know how it was possible, but she must have somehow found out about our missing costumes and decided to take away one of our last remaining options.

"Yes. My apologies. Is there anything else you wanted?"

"No, thanks," I said. "Thanks for your time."

I put down the phone, turning to Mercy as she walked back into the reception area. "You aren't going to believe this."

"What?"

"Janice has hired a theatre group to put on a play at her inn next week, and she already ordered all the local costume shop's stock of reindeer costumes. Every last one of them."

"You're kidding me. Who on earth did she hire to act for her? We already have Marcus's group working for us, and they're not going to turn their backs on us now."

I hope not, whispered a voice in the back of my head. Not only did we have no costumes, we'd lost our backup plan. Coupled with the mysterious transformation of our last order into rabbit costumes of all things, it was seriously starting to look as though someone didn't want the event to go through as planned. Someone like Janice, for instance.

"Supposedly, she hired a new group," I said. "Amateur, but it doesn't matter how good they are if they've already taken all of our costumes, does it? Her goal isn't to put on a show. It's to undermine us."

"How petty can you get? What *is* her problem? Aside from jealousy, I mean."

"I don't know, but do you think she might have been the one to mess with our order?"

"You mean she ambushed the post owl and transformed all our reindeer costumes into rabbits before they got here?" asked Mercy. "I suppose we haven't exactly kept it a secret. If you ask me, the theatre group talked about the play somewhere she could overhear and put the idea in her head."

"Or when she came nosing around here yesterday." Ever since I'd run into her the other day, we'd had nothing but trouble. She hadn't done all this over Mum's misplaced snowball, had she?

"Yeah, but I can't see how she would have known which company we ordered the costumes from or when they were due to be delivered," said Mercy. "Not unless she came in here, which I would definitely have known about."

True. The image of the wishing box came to mind, and my suspicion ratcheted up a notch again. A wishing box would remove the need for her to be present in person to cause trouble for us. Maybe our current deluge of problems was due to magical intervention after all.

"Yeah, maybe I'm overreaching," I said. "Anyway, my parents have been gone for hours. Best case scenario is that they're having too much fun to come back, but I should probably look for them."

"Good idea. I'll stay in and wait for the catering order. Should be here within the hour."

"I'll be back soon. I won't leave you to deal with everything alone."

"I honestly don't mind. Really, we'd be good to go if not for the snowstorm."

And the costume mix-up... not to mention the missing wishing box. Hoping the box *wasn't* the cause of the trouble, I went to track down my parents.

6

I didn't see any signs of Janice outside the inn, but I almost hoped I'd run into her on the way so I could demand to know at which point she'd decided to steal our theatrical production idea and swipe all the reindeer costumes in town.

Admittedly, it was probably for the best that I didn't see her, considering another argument might have made things worse for all of us, but an irritable cloud hung over my head as I walked, and with my attention divided, I nearly walked into Bella coming the other way.

"Whoa." I halted. "There you are. I wondered where you'd disappeared to."

My sister rolled her eyes at me. "Where were you? You were as lost in your own head as Mum and Dad."

"Speaking of whom, whereabouts did they go?" I asked. "I figured I ought to track them down, since they've been gone all day so far."

"No need. They're having the time of their lives at the skating rink. How did your rehearsal go?"

"Fine."

From her raised eyebrows, she could tell from my tone that I hadn't been entirely honest with her. Though the rehearsal itself wasn't what worried me. If we didn't find replacement costumes, there was a good chance Janice might end up enticing the theatre group over to her side after all. Especially if she thought she could offer them a better deal. Not that Bella knew anything about our rivalries with Janice, and to be honest, I preferred to keep it that way.

"I'm glad Mum and Dad found something to do," I added. "I worried about leaving them to their own devices."

"They aren't twelve."

"They act like it sometimes. You know it's true. I thought that's why you came here with them."

"I came here to make sure they found their way to the North Pole in one piece," she said. "They're free to do whatever they like now they're here."

"Within reason. Anyway, are you going back to the inn?"

"Only if it's snow-free."

"It is," I said. "Unless whoever cast the spell comes back, we're good."

"You think someone cast a spell on your inn? Why?"

I shrugged, once again wondering whether to bring up my rivalry with Janice. If she was going to insist on causing trouble for us all week, I might have no choice in the matter, but I could only imagine what would happen if Bella and Janice went head-to-head. It'd make the snowstorm that hit the inn seem like a gentle breeze.

I shook off the thought. "I don't know, but I doubt you

can cast that kind of spell by accident either. Sorry about the snow in your shoes."

She gave a grunt of acknowledgement as she edged around me, which probably meant *you're welcome.*

"Anyway, see you later," I added.

As she left, she shot me a suspicious look, as though she knew perfectly well that I was hiding something from her. All the same, I wasn't about to admit to my sister just how much trouble we might be in. We might be siblings, but we hadn't confided in each other in years. Not since we'd gone on different paths in life. We were just too different.

Now? I wasn't entirely sure if I trusted her or not, especially given her inexplicable decision to follow Mum and Dad on their ridiculous trip to the North Pole when I'd thought she'd find running a marathon with a hangover less unappealing. And now she'd gone and left them to their own devices. Hoping they hadn't got into too much trouble, I headed to the skating rink. It was usually one of my favourite places to go at the weekends after a stressful week, but I doubted I'd get a free moment to have fun until the event was over and my unexpected guests had gone home.

It was easy to spot Mum and Dad's towering hats zooming around the skating rink, and to no one's surprise, they'd drawn attention from everyone in the vicinity as they careened in circles on the smooth, icy surface of the rink. At least nobody was laughing at them. Instead, gasps of astonishment followed their paths as they pirouetted and cavorted and spun one another in circles. I hadn't known they were that good at skating, but they'd even managed to keep their hats attached to their heads while zipping about at the speed of light. Pretty impressive, I had to admit.

Expressions of delight crossed their faces when they spotted me, but I smiled and shook my head to signal that I wasn't coming to join them. The last thing I needed was to fall over and end up breaking a bone right before our event, so I gave them a wave, indicated I was leaving, then left them to it. They didn't seem to mind, resuming their gleeful chasing while I walked away, feeling slightly put out. At least they were enjoying their holiday.

Back at the inn, Bella must have returned to her room because I saw no signs of her downstairs. Instead, I found Mercy in an even more agitated state than she'd been in earlier.

"What's going on?" I asked.

"The ingredients never showed up. My calls aren't going through either. The kitchen staff have nothing to work with."

"What's going on? Is someone screwing with us? Because it's starting to look that way."

"Yes, it is. Did you find your parents, at least?"

"They were having a great time at the rink, so I figured I'd let them carry on until it gets dark," I said. "I never knew they were that good at skating, but they're seriously causing a stir there. In a good way, for once."

"That's a relief. Bella walked in here and looked gloomy as ever. You'd think we hadn't got rid of the snow in her room."

"She hates the cold. She claimed she only came here to keep an eye on our parents, anyway."

The phone rang, and Mercy hastened to answer. "Oh,

hello. Thanks for getting back to me. Whereabouts is the catering… right."

She listened for a moment, her expression stilling in such a way that one of her rare outbursts of anger looked as though it might be on the horizon. "Yes. No, I didn't know. I'm fairly sure we'd have talked about it if we did…"

As they talked, I circled the desk in yet another futile search for our missing wishing box. At this point, I was at a loss to explain where it had ended up, but the number of mishaps stacking up was hard to blame on coincidence alone. My banner had fallen off the wall again in a sad crumpled heap, and I retrieved it with a stifled sigh before laying it down on the desk.

Mercy grew more and more visibly annoyed until she put the phone down. "You aren't going to believe this."

"What?" I asked. "Was that the catering company? Did they say what was taking them so long to deliver the ingredients here?"

"Sounds like they got the wrong address. They delivered the entire order to someone else who's coincidentally running a similar event next week."

"Janice," I said. "She took our order."

She blew out a breath. "Granted, they might have accidentally delivered it to the wrong place, but yes."

I raised a brow. "You sure it's likely to be accidental?"

I mean, we were talking about the person who may or may not have conjured up an inconvenient snowstorm inside our inn, after all.

Her shoulders slumped. "No. Especially after what happened with the costume shop."

"Exactly my thinking." Unfortunately. "Have you heard from the online costume company, anyway?"

"No. I still can't get their form to go through without running into an error message."

Might be more than a computer glitch at work. Simple glitch or not, the fact that two of our orders had wound up in Janice's hands was proof she'd stop at nothing to undercut us. It was about time I tracked her down and cleared things up in person.

I drew in a breath. "If I said I was going to Janice's place to see what she's playing at, would you stop me?"

"Try not to start a fight. Just explain the situation with the ingredients, and she ought to be obligated to hand them over. There's zero chance our orders matched exactly. She might have heard about the costumes from the theatre company, but she couldn't have got hold of our menu. I have the only copy."

"Whereabouts is it?"

"Here." She pushed a laminated piece of paper across the counter at me, and I gave it a scan. "I doubt Janice is going to have the nerve to copy our menu."

"I wouldn't speak too soon," I said, reading the list. "Snowflake cakes, reindeer cookies… did you make all these up?"

"With Angus's help. He won't be thrilled if Janice stole our ideas, either."

"Yeah." The only way she could possibly have known what was on the menu was if she'd taken it from us, but Mercy had had access to our copy the whole time. Unless, of course, she'd used the wishing box.

With the box's magic at her command, Janice could mess up the entire event without even lifting a finger herself. Like it or not, there was no way to have any certainty about that without speaking to her in person.

Tucking the menu underneath my arm, I left the inn. I felt bad leaving Mercy to handle everything alone, but I was the person Janice disliked most of the pair of us, and if something had pushed her over the edge, it was probably the incident with my mother and the snowball. If I had to give her a tongue-lashing over the missing order, I'd rather get it over with before my parents tired of skating, because I definitely didn't need to get them involved with Janice's ridiculous feud. The faster I sorted this out, the better.

At the inn where Janice worked, a festive holly wreath hung on the red-painted door; snow fringed the windowsills; and a near-exact imitation of our own collection of realistic-looking snow witches sat on either side of the doors. To add insult to injury, several boxes from the local catering company were stacked in the lobby, as if she'd intended to rub them in my face.

Janice herself glanced up from behind the desk when I walked in, wearing a fake smile and putting on an equally fake customer service voice. "Can I help you with… oh, it's you." The smile and simper vanished on the spot, to be replaced with her customary scowl.

I suppressed an eye roll. "Yes, it's me. I think our catering order somehow ended up at your address."

"Excuse me?" she said. "The order that showed up is exactly what I ordered for my event next week."

"You happened to order the exact same items as on this menu, which we put together weeks ago?" I held up the piece of laminated paper. "Snowflake cakes, reindeer cookies... I don't see any other places serving those particular snacks."

Her gaze skimmed over the menu. "You don't have a monopoly on all the Christmas-themed menus in town, you know."

"I'm aware of that," I said testily. "We wrote the menu weeks ago, and the ingredients were due to show up at our place today."

"I thought you'd already placed the order."

"We had to place a second one because someone made it snow all over the inn and drenched all the ingredients in melted snow. Know anything about that?"

She blinked. "Snow? Isn't it always snowing?"

"Hilarious." Apparently, she'd decided to opt for outright denial. "Also, the rabbit costumes were overkill. Just so you know."

"What rabbit costumes?" She sounded baffled, as though she had no idea what I was talking about, but I wasn't fooled for an instant.

"You know exactly what I mean," I said. "Look, the event is going ahead. We've been preparing for weeks, and we've already sold half our tickets. All you're doing by trying to sabotage us at this point is making a lot of people mad at you."

"I have no idea what you're talking about."

She sounded almost genuine, but she had some nerve feigning ignorance when she was the one who'd swiped all the reindeer costumes from the costume shop *and* taken our catering order. Why shouldn't she also have been responsible for the blizzard, the rabbit costume fiasco, and our inability to get through to the online shop using either the phone or their online form as well? Nobody else would have the audacity, surely.

"Sure you don't," I said. "I take it I'm not going to walk out of here and find you've taken our choir next?"

"You don't own them."

My irritation peaked. "We *do* own a certain valuable magical object that went missing from our property yesterday."

Her blank expression didn't falter. "What?"

Oh, come on. How could I get the wishing box out of her hands when she was studiously denying any wrongdoing? Short of searching the place without her knowing, that is, and stealth was not my forte. Stealing wasn't appealing, either, though she'd done the exact same when she'd taken the wishing box to begin with.

I shook my head. "Never mind. If you want to send us our order back, you know our address."

I left before my mouth got me into even more trouble, my annoyance mingling with my growing confusion. It seemed she *didn't* know about the box, but who else could be responsible for our misfortune? The boxes full of the ingredients Mercy and I had paid for were sitting right there on her property. No, she must have been honing her acting skills to feign ignorance.

"Carolyn?" said a voice from behind me.

I spun around, my heart sinking when I saw my parents meandering towards me, hats bobbing on their heads.

"Who was that?" asked Mum. "And why do those snow witches look like the ones outside your inn?"

"No one," I said. "I was paying someone a visit."

"It sounded like you were having an argument."

I felt my resolve weakening by the second. I hadn't wanted to tell my parents of our recent misfortune, but if Janice chose to strike again, maybe I'd be better off warning them in advance.

"You know I mentioned we were having an event this weekend?" I said. "Janice is prone to 'borrowing' our ideas, and she's taken it a bit too far this time. She decided to buy all the reindeer costumes in town, and now our catering order has mysteriously ended up on her doorstep instead of ours."

"Well, that's just not fair," Mum said.

"Absolutely not," Dad said. "You paid for the order, right?"

"The catering, we did, but Mercy is working on it. The costumes, she got before we had the chance to buy them, so there's nothing we can do about those."

"I'll talk to her," said Mum, as though I was back at school and she was prepared to march in and complain to the teachers when she'd heard I was being bullied by the other kids. Needless to say, her intervention hadn't made the teasing stop. In fact, it'd got far worse. I'd stopped telling my parents that kind of thing out of self-preservation, and now I remembered why.

"Wait a moment," I said hastily. "She denied everything. We have no proof."

"But you said she took your order?" asked Dad. "The one you paid for? Is that right?"

"The catering company delivered our order to her instead because she copied our menu," I explained. "She might not be responsible for the mix-up, though, so Mercy and I are going to speak directly to the catering company to clear it up. We don't need any more stress."

"Of course not," Mum said. "I understand, sweetheart. Are you going back to the inn now?"

"Yes," I said firmly. "Come on, let's go. You can tell me what you've been up to today on the way back."

Now all I had to do was hope that telling them about Janice's scheming didn't end up being a huge mistake.

7

I walked back to the inn with both my parents, who talked excitedly about their escapades of the day. From what I gathered, they'd skated for hours with a break for lunch at a local cafe and were now buzzing with enthusiasm about unpacking the souvenirs they'd bought from the market to add to the piles of tinsel they'd acquired yesterday. I opted against asking how on earth they planned to get everything home.

"Is Bella around?" Mum asked as we neared the inn.

"Ah, yeah, she came back earlier," I said. "The blizzard has stopped, by the way. The snow in your room's probably melted."

"Oh," said Dad. "We can clean up the room, no problem. It was fun while it lasted."

"Yes, it was," Mum agreed. "I suppose the other guests didn't like it much."

"No, they really didn't." Especially Bella, who wasn't a fan of the cold wet stuff in the slightest. "I think I prefer our snow witches to stay outside the inn."

"That reminds me," Mum said. "I want to get a picture outside with your wonderful sculptures."

"Excellent idea," said Dad. "Let's do it now."

They ambled over to the collection of snow witches outside the doors while I ducked inside the inn. There, I found Mercy perched on a stepladder, in the middle of affixing my banner back above the door to the hall. She'd somehow managed to fix the damage from the melted snow so it looked as pristine as it had when I'd first put it up.

"You didn't have to do that."

"You worked really hard on the banner." She finished positioning it over the door frame and stepped off the ladder. "I couldn't see it all go to waste."

"How're you getting on with the catering company?" I placed the laminated menu back on the front desk. "Any luck getting through to them on the phone?"

"Better than with the costume shop." She folded up the ladder and stashed it back behind the desk. "Turns out we didn't get charged for the order. What did Janice have to say for herself, then?"

"She said she coincidentally happened to have the same menu we did. Snowflake cakes and all."

"She didn't." A flush swept over her cheeks. "I can't believe she said that to your face."

"She even had the nerve to act as though she didn't have a clue what I was talking about when I mentioned everything else that's gone wrong," I added. "I probably shouldn't have, but the costume thing is doubly annoying because it's hard to prove she did anything wrong. We originally ordered ours online, after all, not from the local shop."

"Exactly. That doesn't get her off the hook, though. Not in the slightest. She *did* take our catering order."

"Did you tell them that on the phone?"

"Yes, but I'm not sure they believed me." She picked up the menu again. "They said I'll have to call back tomorrow to reorder everything we need. Janice bought the whole lot."

"Of course she did." I rolled my eyes. "You know, between that and the costumes, I'm not going to be surprised if Janice leaps in to steal the carollers from in front of our eyes at tonight's rehearsal."

I'd forgotten all about the choir rehearsal that evening, for the most part, but at least the local carollers weren't known for being as melodramatic and demanding as Marcus. All we needed to do was give them a place to stand and sing, and they'd be perfectly happy.

"She's not going to steal the choir, Carol," said Mercy, though she didn't sound a hundred percent certain. "Besides, if she *is* the person messing with us, she's spent more time on that than doing any actual planning for her own event. She'll have to leave us alone if she wants to avoid humiliating herself next week."

"Maybe," I said, "but if she took the wishing box, she can accomplish anything without having to actually make all the calls herself."

"You think? She's certainly capable of doing all this without access to the box, you know."

"I guess. It would explain how she got our menu, though. She was one step ahead of us. Nobody else could have given it to her, could they?"

"I have no idea," she said. "Unless she asked the

catering company herself and they told her. I didn't tell them not to share the details."

"Typical." My annoyance levels spiked. "I tried to get her to confess to stealing it, but she refused to so much as admit she knew it existed. I'd rather not have provoked her any further, especially if she did turn out to have the wishing box hidden somewhere on her property."

"Yeah, that might turn nasty," she said. "I think she's definitely behind the mix-up with the orders. I'm not sure if she'd have needed magic to do it, that's all."

I rubbed my forehead. "If she *does* have the wishing box, then how are we supposed to get it back? I didn't see it when I walked into the inn, but it's not like I can search every room without her catching me. Besides, the idea of stealing it back… that has the potential to backfire on all of us if we can't prove the box was ours to begin with."

"Who's stealing what?" Bella walked over to the desk, looking between us with a distinct expression of suspicion on her face. Which reminded me: Mum and Dad still hadn't returned from taking photos of themselves with the collection of snow witches outside. Maybe they'd become distracted with another snowball fight.

"Nothing," I said. "Our catering order ended up at the wrong place."

"Yes, Mum and Dad said," she said. "That's why they went to talk to what's-her-name. Whoever you were arguing with earlier. I just ran into them outside, and they said they were going to sort her out."

"They said *what?*" Oh no. "I told them not to go and start an argument with Janice. I *told* them."

"Why did you tell them anything at all?" asked my sister. "You must have known they wouldn't be able to stop themselves from intervening. They have all the self-control of a pair of five-year-olds in a confectionary shop."

Oh, god, they went after Janice.

"I told them because they saw me arguing with her and I didn't have a cover story planned." I made for the door, grabbing my coat on the way out. "I'll catch them up."

I'd hoped they wouldn't have gone far, but my parents could move fast when they wanted to, and they'd already vanished from sight by the time I skidded to a halt at the end of the road. Cursing under my breath, I broke into a sprint towards Janice's inn.

I came to a breathless halt outside, knowing I was far too late. Mum and Dad were already inside, and judging by the sound of raised voices, they'd wasted no time in lecturing Janice over the missing order. If I went in there and dragged them out, it'd be just as humiliating as letting them say their piece, and likely with the same result—but leaving them wasn't an option, either.

Janice's voice drifted out through a gap in the door. "If you don't tell me what I'm supposed to have done wrong, then I'm calling the police."

Oh, boy. She probably would, too, and I didn't need to spend the rest of the week trying to get my parents out of jail at the North Pole. I'd prefer not to end up in a cell of my own, come to that. Poor Mercy didn't deserve to end up having to run the event alone while I argued with the local law enforcement over my parents' antics.

Mentally bracing myself, I went into the building and found my parents facing Janice across the front desk. She wore her customary glower, but neither of my parents seemed fazed in the slightest. "I can't believe you have the nerve to come in here and accuse me of stealing on my own property."

"This is Carolyn and Mercy's order," Mum said loudly, pointing to the boxes stacked near the doors. "You stole it from them."

"I did not," Janice said. "Besides, I wrote the menu myself."

"Oh, come on," I interjected. "We both know that's nonsense. Mercy wrote the menu in conjunction with our kitchen staff. We have the proof that we were the first to place the order, before an incident involving an indoor snowstorm ruined it."

She wheeled on me. "Oh, really? What proof do you have, exactly?"

"The receipt for the original order, for a start." She must know she was fighting a losing battle here. "I watched Mercy write the menu, and I don't need to be a genius to see something is amiss here."

"Exactly," Dad said. "Carolyn has been working hard on this event. I'm disappointed to see people are out to take advantage of her."

"She's the one who's taking advantage!" Janice insisted, but her tone was half-hearted enough to surprise me. I hadn't expected her to give in easily, but I doubted she'd ever been confronted by a couple of oddly dressed people wearing strange hats before. She didn't seem to know how to handle them. "Besides, the boxes are already here."

"We made the same order, but ours was due today," I countered. "Unless you travelled back in time, that is. If I let you keep the boxes for yourself, that won't change the basic fact that our event is going to take place before yours."

"Exactly," Mum said. "You were threatening to call the police, but she has the evidence, not you."

Janice looked between us, her face flushing. She knew she'd been backed into a corner, and while it surprised me a little that she didn't retaliate, perhaps she was concerned about the kind of magic a pair of people with magically created hats might be able to cast on her.

"Oh, fine," she said. "Take the boxes yourself if it means that much to you."

"Excellent," said Dad. "That's all we wanted. Thank you very much for cooperating."

Janice looked utterly lost for words, possibly for the first time in her life, when Mum beamed at her before making her way over to the stack of boxes by the door.

As Mum and Dad moved to pick up the boxes between them, I hastened to say, "I'll call the catering company to fetch them, don't worry. Come on, let's get out of here."

I tried not to let a pleading note enter my voice. Janice's expression was furious, if still embarrassed and wary on top of it, and I wouldn't put it past her to use her magic on us all when our backs were turned. She rarely used her elemental magic in public, but I'd never seen her this mad before.

I let my parents leave the inn first and then followed, releasing a sigh of relief when we made it to the street's end without Janice throwing a giant snowball at us in return for her humiliation.

"Good," Mum said, sounding incredibly pleased with herself. "That's that sorted. She won't bother you again."

"I wouldn't speak too soon," I said. "Janice has been out to get us since we opened our inn, and I'm fairly sure she conjured up the snowstorm earlier too."

"She did?" said Dad. "Why didn't you say so?"

"Can you please not go after her again?" I looked between them. "Let's wait until after the event is done before causing any more trouble. I have to help the catering company bring in the boxes, and I can't do that if either of you is in jail."

"Of course, sweetheart," said Mum. "We don't want to ruin your big day."

Thankfully, they returned to the inn without a fuss and without Janice appearing from a snowdrift and using her magic on us. Admittedly, she wouldn't need to do so if she did turn out to have the wishing box… a possibility I didn't really want to think about now we'd royally ticked her off. Maybe we should have asked where she'd hidden the wishing box while she'd been in a contrite mood, but that might have been pushing it too far.

Mercy raised her eyebrows at me as I walked into the inn, but I waited for my parents to go back to their rooms before explaining the new developments to her.

"We got the order back," I said. "The catering, I mean."

"Seriously?" Her face lit up. "Where is it?"

"Still at Janice's place, but I'll call the catering company to go and pick it up," I said. "Janice said I could."

"She did? What on earth did your parents do to her?"

"Told her they were disappointed in her."

Mercy burst into laughter. "I wish I'd seen her face. That's priceless."

"Yeah, but I'm not going to stop watching my back just yet. She might end up sneakily putting snow inside the boxes before they get here."

"Would she bother with that now she knows you can

send your parents back to intimidate her again?" She chuckled under her breath.

"It won't help if she douses our ingredients in another snowstorm," I reminded her. "And if she does turn out to have the wishing box, she has the ability to do much worse."

"Maybe, but I'm not sure she does have it," she said. "She could have done worse than conjuring up a snowstorm... not that I'm looking to tempt fate, mind you, but it's true."

"Yeah, she didn't do anything which might have had a magical cause aside from the snowstorm," I allowed. "Now, though? She's really mad at us."

"We'll be on our guard, then. Anyway, I'll call the catering company. You let the chef know the order's on its way."

"Will do."

While she picked up the phone, I headed to the kitchen to let the staff know about the upcoming order. Angus the chef accosted me at the door. "Any sign of our order yet? Janet tried to steal it, did she?"

"She didn't succeed," I said. "The catering company will be bringing it here shortly. Also, it's Janice, not Janet, but I'd like to see her face if you called her that."

He grinned. "I'd like to have seen her face after you snatched our order back from her. Anyway, thanks for letting me know. Your snowflake cakes and reindeer cookies will be right on schedule."

"Thanks." While relief washed over me at the notion of our menu being saved, I tamped down my enthusiasm as I returned to the reception area to wait for the boxes to show up, hoping Janice hadn't sabotaged anything. Luckily, it seemed her confrontation with my parents had momentarily cowed her. The boxes arrived without delay, and when we checked, not a single snowflake was in sight.

The costumes, however, remained as much of a dead end as before. Janice might have relinquished her control over one aspect of our event, but she still had the costume shop's entire supply of reindeer costumes, and we had yet to find a replacement, with the online form resolutely refusing to cooperate. I sincerely hoped Marcus got over his tantrum, because asking the choir to learn everyone's lines before the weekend didn't seem plausible.

"I don't know. It's worth a shot," said Mercy, when I said this aloud. "At least they have the singing parts down."

"That, or we find the wishing box and wish for a way out of this." I couldn't believe I hadn't seen a single sign of it yet. "We can wish for the costumes to show up… or maybe we should just wish for the whole thing to go ahead without a hitch in order to cover all our bases. Because it feels like someone else is wishing for the opposite."

"Yeah, it does. Or we've wandered into a wicked stream of bad luck."

"True." We still had to get through the choir's rehearsal this evening, and I was starting to think that looking for the wishing box might be a safer bet than attempting to mitigate each disaster one at a time. The box was the one solution that could solve all our problems, but if it was in Janice's hands, how on earth would we get her to admit it?

8

Despite the lingering shadow of Janice's anger, I found myself looking forward to that night's choir rehearsal. It seemed my parents had worn themselves out with their energetic day at the ice rink and didn't decide to go back for Round Two with Janice, to my relief. While they went into the restaurant for the evening meal, Mercy and I grabbed a quick dinner to eat at the desk while we waited for the carollers to show up.

As I predicted, the first group of carollers showed up at eight on the dot, greeting me with a loud rendition of "Hark! The Herald Angels Sing." Red hats bounced on their heads, and jingling bells hung around their necks. The choir always wore their own costumes, so there was no need to worry about any more delivery disasters, and they were much easier to handle than Marcus. Aside from the singing, which got a bit much sometimes, they were no trouble whatsoever.

Inevitably, the noise drew my parents out of the

restaurant. They goggled openly at the carollers, confusion turning to delight when the newcomers finished their verse and walked into the hall to prepare for the rehearsal.

"What's going on?" Mum asked me.

"We're doing another rehearsal," I said. "For the carollers who are going to sing during the intervals of the play this Saturday."

"Oh, that sounds like fun!" she said. "Can we watch?"

"Ah…" I hesitated. "Okay, why not."

My parents might be an overenthusiastic audience, but the carollers were hard to faze. They were pretty much trained to get on with the show, rain or shine. Even if the audience was pelting them with tomatoes, they kept on singing.

"Excellent," said Dad. "I'll ask Bella if she wants to come and watch too."

I had my sincere doubts Bella would be in the least bit interested, but it might bolster the carollers' enthusiasm to have an audience. It'd also help them forget about Janice and her vendetta, too, which was a bonus.

After my parents had departed, I heard Bella's voice drift out of the restaurant. "Why would I want to listen to people sing carols? I've heard practically nothing else all day."

Thought so.

While the carollers continued to show up in small groups, Bella stalked off to her room without acknowledging their presence. No surprise there. Even they might have a tough time staying upbeat with Bella glowering at them, so it was probably for the best that she stayed away from the rehearsal. The carollers ranged from young to old, with all manner of talent levels, but all that was required to join their group was a high level of enthusiasm. Larry, their unofficial leader, accompanied the third group of carollers. The elf wore a bright-green-and-red-striped hat sitting between his pointed ears which rivalled one of my parents' creations for sheer extravagance.

"Hey," I said to Larry. "Is everyone ready?"

"Yes." His usual smile was absent, replaced with a rather harried expression. "Sorry for the delay… someone decided to move all our costumes out of the rehearsal studio and stuck them in a cupboard instead. Also, you should know, Janice asked us to come and sing at her event next week. It was only when we realised that the rehearsals would clash with your event that we said no."

My mouth fell open. *She actually did try to recruit our carollers?*

"Shame to turn down the cash, though," put in one of the others.

"Why, what does she want you to do for her?" Was she already trying to get me back for the humiliation she'd experienced at my parents' hands earlier, since we'd managed to wrangle our stolen ingredient delivery from her hands?

"Sounds like she's putting on a play of her own next week," said Larry. "She told us she needs a choir for the intervals."

"Does she, now?" Mercy said in displeased tones. "You weren't tempted, were you?"

"Some of the carollers were, but I'm sure you'll have enough of us left over for your event."

I hope so. The local choir was a large group, so we could spare a handful of people. In fact, a smaller group might be easier to manage. Getting everyone in line on the stage was like herding cats, which became almost literal when Charlie, Mum's familiar, ran across the stage and nearly caused several people to topple off the platform. Mum bounded forward to scoop him up with an apology and returned to her seat at the front of the hall.

"Oh, I didn't know we had an audience," said Larry.

"Is that okay?" I hovered at the side of the stage, trying my best to focus on the carollers and not on my parents' presence in the front row. "My parents are visiting for a few days, and they wanted to watch your rehearsal. They won't disturb you." As long as Mum kept her cat under close watch, anyway.

"Of course." His sunny smile returned. "We'll have to make our performance the best that we possibly can, then."

Once the choir had got themselves properly organised, they launched into the actual rehearsal. I had to admit I was proud of their sheer enthusiasm. They sang loudly enough to make the stage vibrate underfoot, and it wouldn't surprise me if their voices could be heard upstairs too. I half-expected Bella to storm in here and demand that they go outside, though she'd complained much less during her trip than I might have expected. Though that might change if the choir didn't have to keep stopping to start the first verse of "Silent Night" from the beginning. The downside to having so many people onstage was that when someone made a mistake, it was hard to pinpoint the source. As it turned out, some of the carollers had different ideas about singing in tune than others did.

Mum and Dad sat politely through it all with minimal

commentary, but each verse sounded worse than the last until even the ever-optimistic Larry couldn't ignore it any longer.

"Who keeps making that croaking noise?" he asked. "It's very distracting."

Nobody said anything. Larry scanned the assembled choir, his usual friendly demeanour beginning to dim. "Okay, start from the beginning."

They broke into song, but once again, a discordant croaking interrupted their verse.

"Stop!" Larry said. "What was that?"

"Him." Dad pointed into the group. "It's him."

"He's a frog!" Mum announced loudly.

Oh, boy. I faced my parents and mouthed, "Mum, please be quiet."

"I mean he really is a frog," she said, jabbing a finger at the group. "Look."

As I peered across the stage, some of the carollers shuffled to the side to reveal a frog sitting in place of one of their number.

"Isn't that Bertrand?" asked Larry. "Which of you turned him into a frog?"

A chorus of accusations and exclamations rose up among the carollers as everyone started pointing fingers at one another. Someone picked up the frog to remove him from the stage, and poor Bertrand didn't like that in the slightest. With a loud croak, he leapt from his captor's hands and hopped underneath a chair.

Then another yell came from the other end of the line of carollers. "Casey turned into a frog too!"

"Who's doing this?" Larry's voice echoed throughout the hall, while the carollers' formation broke up as everyone began looking wildly around for the culprit. As they scattered, two more of them turned into large green frogs, sitting in puddles of cloak which were suddenly far too big for them. Panicked shouts ensued, interspersed with loud croaking as one by one, the others succumbed to the spell. The ongoing confusion made it even harder to see the culprit.

"Wait!" Larry ran along the stage, trying to herd the others back into the line, but every passing second brought more croaking until the frogs outnumbered the humans and the noise grew to deafening levels.

I hopped off the stage and ran to Mercy's side, where she stood staring in horror at the chaos. "I can't see who's doing this. It can't be one of the carollers."

"I'm not sure they're even here in the hall. I'll look outside."

"Careful to avoid getting hit by the spell," I warned her. Whoever was doing this had either hidden themselves somehow or they were acting from outside the inn.

As Mercy left the hall, I ran past the seats, peering under each row to see if anyone was hiding underneath. Aside from my parents, though, nobody else showed up. Larry's attempts to get the choir in line grew more and more half-hearted until he finally turned into a frog too.

When Larry fell into a croaking heap, I ran towards the stage, as if I could do anything to stop it. By the time I caught up, though, the last handful of carollers' voices had turned to nothing but croaking. I looked in horror at the mass of croaking green frogs that covered the stage, sitting in piles of discarded clothes and shoes. Every single member of the choir had been transformed into amphibians.

At that moment, Mercy came running back into the hall. At least she wasn't a frog too. "Nobody is outside," she told me.

"Then…" It must have been caused by the wishing box. There was no other way for a spell to hit that many people at once, not without the caster even being in the room. "Janice strikes again."

Mum and Dad stood up and clapped, drawing our attention to the front row.

"What are you doing?" I asked.

"Wasn't that supposed to happen?" asked Mum.

My mouth fell open. "Of course not. Someone cast a spell on the choir."

Someone, for instance, who they'd recently humiliated into giving back the boxes she'd swiped from our catering company.

"Was it her?" Dad said. "The one we spoke with earlier?"

Mum's gaze went unusually sharp, and my heart sank. I hadn't expected them to be that quick on the uptake, but if Janice had been behind the carollers' transformation, I did not want my parents to join them. Besides, if it *was* Janice, it was their interference earlier that'd caused her latest prank.

"I have no idea," I said instead. "We need to turn everyone back before the weekend or we can say goodbye to our event. Do you have any idea how to undo a spell like this?"

"I know a transforming spell," Mum said. "I haven't tried it on a person before."

"I think it only works on hats," Dad said.

"Better not try it." If Mum and Dad tried to undo the

spell, the odds were high that they'd end up turning the frogs into toads or something. The only magic they were good at involved hats. Unfortunately, my own magic was even less useful in this situation.

Mercy eyed the stage, her expression bleak. "I don't know how to undo the spell, especially if it's the result of a wishing box. Janice has really done it this time."

"You think it was definitely her, then?" I murmured.

"Yeah. It's obvious."

Too bad she hadn't shown her face in person, instead leaving us to deal with the aftermath by ourselves. As much as I wanted to confront her, we couldn't just leave the frogs sitting onstage for however long it took for them to turn back. Some of them might escape and freeze to death outside or get caught by Mum's familiar. We needed to find somewhere to put them.

"What are we supposed to do with the frogs while we wait for a solution?" I asked. "This place isn't exactly friendly to amphibians. Especially if it starts snowing in here again."

"I guess we can put them in the dressing room," Mercy said. "Frogs don't take up much space. Besides, they used to be human, so they're probably more resilient than regular frogs. They should be fine spending the night in there."

There didn't seem to be a better option, so we returned to the stage. While we were trying to herd the frogs away from their discarded cloaks and towards the dressing room, Bella walked into the hall, raising her brows. "What is going on in here?"

"Someone decided it was funny to turn the choir into frogs," I said.

Amusement flickered across her features. "Did they? Maybe I should have stayed down to watch after all."

"It's not funny," I said. "If we can't turn them back before the weekend, then we're screwed."

"I'm sure they'll turn back of their own accord," she said. "Like the snowstorm."

"That's by no means a guarantee." What made her so certain about the time frame? I thought of the wishing box, and a sudden jolt of suspicion hit me. She hadn't been telling the truth when she'd said she hadn't known we had it, because I'd seen her attention flicker towards the box when Mercy had been stashing it in the back room. What if that wasn't the only thing she'd lied about? It'd crossed my mind at first that she might have taken the box to mess with me, but I'd dismissed that theory when it seemed she'd come here out of genuine concern for our parents after all. I wouldn't have thought to blame her for the snowstorm, regardless, but she'd made no secret of how much she hated the choir's singing. Still, Janice was the far more likely culprit, and Bella wouldn't take kindly to an unfounded accusation.

Mercy glanced over at my sister. "Can you watch the door to make sure none of them get out?"

Without waiting for an answer, I returned to helping Mercy capture the frogs. My parents supplied the surprisingly helpful suggestion of scooping the frogs into their hats to transport them across the hall. Since neither of them seemed to mind us using their hats for that purpose, we managed to get the situation somewhat under control. The frogs weren't happy with the arrangement in the slightest, but it was that or spend the whole night herding them around.

With the frogs finally ensconced in the back room, there was little for us to do but wait until morning and cross our fingers that they turned back into humans overnight. Or until their families started calling our landline, wondering why they hadn't come home yet. It'd take all night to call everyone's relatives to inform them of the unfortunate turn of events, though, and it wouldn't be worth causing widespread panic if they turned back into humans within a few hours anyway.

"I'm sure their families won't be too worried," Mercy said when I mentioned this, closing the door on the back room. In the absence of the frogs' discordant croaking, silence fell over the hall at last. "They're usually out half the night singing, aren't they?"

"I don't know about letting the event go ahead even if they do turn back, though," I admitted. "This is one disaster too many. I thought we might be able to get around the issue with the costumes if we asked the choir to take the place of any members of the theatre company who want to drop out, but we can't do that if they're all frogs."

"I know. I thought Marcus might come around about the costumes, but if he and the rest of their group find out we have a chorus of frogs for a choir, then they'll back out for sure."

"Great." I released a sigh, watching my parents out of the corner of my eye. Their hats were back in place, and I sincerely hoped neither of them had accidentally picked up one of the frogs as a hitchhiker. That would get awkward if they turned back into humans, to say the least.

My parents approached us, their expressions unusually sombre. I guessed they'd realised just how much trouble we were in.

"What's going on with the costumes?" asked Dad.

"Didn't I tell you? *Someone* switched out our reindeer costumes for rabbit ones, and we can't get through to the online company to reorder them in time for the event. Meanwhile, Janice bought the local shop's entire supply of reindeer costumes, so we have no alternative. Not that it matters at this rate. Would you want to take part in an event when someone keeps pranking everyone involved?"

"We can help with the costumes," Mum offered. "I'm pretty sure we have at least one reindeer hat among our collection. And if not, then we can make one."

"We need a dozen, not one. Anyway, it's not your…"

I trailed off, since I didn't quite know how I'd intended to end that sentence. *You're supposed to be on holiday,* I wanted to say, but also, *It's our job. We're supposed to be dealing with this by ourselves.*

Then again, given how little time we had until the event started, it was probably better to let them help out rather than risk the show not being able to go ahead at all. Why shouldn't I let my family do what they did best? If they salvaged the situation for all of us in the process, so much the better.

"We can help," Dad agreed. "It's no trouble for us."

I relented. "Okay. If you really want to make a dozen reindeer hats by the weekend when you're supposed to be on holiday, then feel free."

At least they'd be distracted from picking a fight with Janice again, but a sinking feeling in my chest warned me that the frogs might not be the end of it. For all we knew, she wouldn't be satisfied until every single one of our plans lay in tatters around us. One thing was clear: we needed to find the real source of the trouble and bring it to a halt before the weekend.

As Mum and Dad left, I spotted Charlie the cat padding across the hall.

"Hey, you can't go out there." I followed him towards the emergency exit, where he pushed the door open to reveal the alley around the back of the inn. I caught the door before it closed, watching as Charlie nudged open one of the old recycling bins we'd stashed around the back. Inside the bin lay a collection of small coins and other items that I assumed the cat had sneaked out of the inn. It seemed he'd been busy while my parents were out, but I'd forgotten about his tendency to hoard random objects and hide them.

"Sorry, Charlie, but you're going to have to spend the night indoors." I reached out and picked him up, grimacing when he dug his claws into my arm. "Don't look at me like that. I'm not going to spend tomorrow calling the choir's family members to tell them that my mother's cat ate them while they were trapped in the back room as amphibians."

Charlie squirmed in my grip until I caught up with my parents on the stairs and released him.

"Can you keep him in your room overnight?" I asked Mum. "I don't want him figuring out how to open the dressing room door and getting at the frogs."

"Oh, good thinking." She caught Charlie, who made a small noise of annoyance as she carried him over to the door to the room. "I'll make sure he doesn't get out."

"He keeps stealing things and putting them outside," I

added. "He's using one of our recycling bins to store his hoard in."

"Oh, I know. You remember he used to do the same when you lived at home, right?"

"Yes..." I trailed off. "He did."

Charlie liked collecting bright and shiny magical treasures, and the wishing box definitely fit those criteria. Had he taken the wishing box from the back room to add to his hoard too? If he'd hidden it in the recycling bin and left the lid open, then it would have been a simple matter for someone who'd happened across his hiding place to take it for their own. Someone, say, who'd been spying on the inn from nearby.

This time, Janice, we've got you.

9

Holding onto my patience throughout the night while we waited to confront Janice took all the willpower I possessed. It didn't help that I kept expecting to wake up to another snowstorm or some other disaster that had fallen upon us while we slept. Early the following morning, I went downstairs to check on the choir in the hopes that the frog spell had worn off. Oh, and to make sure Charlie hadn't eaten any of them. I'd hope he'd have more sense, but you never really knew.

"They're still frogs," Mercy said dismally from behind the front desk, looking as tired as I felt. "I checked. We're going to have to tell their families ASAP unless we can find some way to turn them back into humans again within the next few hours. Not to mention keep them safe from the cat."

My heart sank when I spotted Charlie wandering around the reception area, having probably slipped out of my parents' room the instant my mum turned her back. "Has he been near the back room?"

"He tried. That's why I've been sitting here for the last hour."

"I think he's the one who initially took the wishing box. I forgot he has a habit of hoarding shiny things, but he's been building quite the stash in one of the recycling bins around the back of the inn. He'd have been quite capable of sneaking into the back room and swiping it while I was showing my parents around town."

Her eyes rounded. "You think so?"

"If he did take it, anyone might have swiped it from his hiding spot," I added. "We know Janice was hanging around here more or less at the same time as it vanished. If he left the recycling bin open, she'd have spotted its glittering gemstones a mile off."

"Sounds plausible," said Mercy, "but we don't have long left if we're going to get it back before the event starts, and we can't prove where it ended up after it disappeared from Charlie's hiding place."

"True." I tailed the cat to the back door again in the hopes of getting a better look around in daylight, but it was obvious the wishing box wasn't in the recycling bin. Not anymore, in any case. Worse, Janice would even be able to claim she hadn't stolen it but had simply found it lying around—which was, technically, true.

I returned to the inn, finding that Mum, Dad, and Bella had come downstairs for breakfast. Only Bella looked well-rested out of the three of them, though Mum and Dad wore cheerful expressions despite the dark circles under their eyes.

Mum carried a half-made hat with antlers on it and placed it on the counter in front of a bewildered Mercy.

"We worked on making the new hats for hours," she said.

"I did tell you not to stay up late on our account," I protested.

"Oh, it was fun," Dad said brightly. "Come upstairs and see the rest, won't you?"

"All right."

I obligingly followed them upstairs to their room, where it couldn't be more obvious that Mum and Dad had worked hard at putting the hats together for hours. Hats sat in a row on the desk, topped with antlers of various sizes, many of them attached to hoods which would go perfectly with the costumes we already had if we removed the rabbit ears.

Mum held out the antlers she'd been showing to Mercy. "Look. I think this is our best one."

I took the antlers from her and examined them. I had to admit she'd done a great job. Better than the costume shop, even. But would that be enough for Marcus?

"I like it," I said. "Should I take the ones you've finished downstairs?"

"Go ahead." She reached out for the antlers and piled them into my arms.

Laden with antlers, I went to show Mercy, whose expression brightened at the sight of my cargo. "Wow, they've been busy."

"I know." I placed the pile of antlers on the counter and extracted a pair. "Do you think this would pass Marcus's inspection, if we combined it with one of the rabbit costumes and replaced the bunny ears with antlers?"

"You know, I think it would. I'll call the theatre group

right away and tell them we have replacements for their costumes. If they agree to press on with the event without further delay, I can stop trying to contact the costume shop. I never did manage to get that form of theirs to go through."

"Sure, go ahead. I'll fetch the rabbit costumes."

Firstly, I counted out how many hats Mum and Dad had actually managed to make. Enough for at least half the group, by the look of things. Not bad at all. If they spent the day working on the rest, then we might just have enough to cover everyone in the theatre group with plenty of time before the event started. Assuming Janice didn't turn them into squirrels anyway, of course.

Argh. I have to deal with her. We were so close to the event that Janice would have limited chances to strike again, so I'd need to figure out a way to stop her from interfering.

The universe had other plans. Not five minutes after Mercy had hung up from speaking to the theatre group, Marcus himself entered the reception area.

"What's this I'm hearing about a new costume?" he asked.

Mercy stared at him. "Were you already walking here when I was talking to you on the phone?"

"I was in the area, yes. Some of the others are on their way here too. I told them you had new costumes ready for us."

Oh, no. I hadn't planned for the theatre group to come here immediately, before we'd got all their costumes together… and before we'd cleared the frogs out of their changing room.

"We're still working on the costumes." I held the

antlers up in demonstration. "We have a few ready. If you put these on as well as the rabbit costumes and then tuck away the bunny ears, nobody will know."

"Is that your professional advice?" he said incredulously.

"It's all we have," said Mercy. "If you want to buy reindeer costumes from the local shop instead, there's a three-week waiting list and we'd have to ask everyone in your group to chip in towards the costs. The antlers we have will work just fine."

"Let me see that." He took them from me, holding the antlers up to the light. "I suppose this is adequate."

It's better than what you had before. At least he hadn't outright said no. One thing had to be said for my parents: when it came to anything hat-related, they were always at the top of their game. Even Marcus had no complaints about their overnight handiwork. I took the antlers from him and put them back with the others.

Marcus's gaze went to the desk. "There are only six pairs. Where are the other costumes?"

"Ah, they're not all ready yet," Mercy said. "We have a team working around the clock on making enough antlers for your entire group. If we have your approval, we can have the rest done within the next day."

"I'll give my approval once someone tries them on to make sure there aren't any issues."

He clearly wasn't volunteering himself, no doubt because of the humiliation of ending up in a rabbit costume last time. Regardless of whoever volunteered, though, we needed to get rid of the frogs before the theatre group could use their changing room.

"Feel free to take one of the costumes home with you to try on," I ventured. "Then the others can come back when the rest of the costumes are ready."

"No need," said Marcus. "They're already here."

Mercy and I scarcely had the chance to exchange alarmed glances before the door opened and Daryl walked in along with a group of other theatre group members. As usual, he went brick red when he spotted Mercy. "What's going on in here?"

Marcus held out a pair of antlers towards Daryl. "These are part of our new reindeer costumes. One of you has to volunteer to try one of them on to make sure there aren't any potential issues."

Daryl examined the new set of antlers. "Okay, I'll do it. Should I change in the back again?"

I glanced at Mercy. "We're using that room for something else."

"Yes, we are," she said. "You can change in the hall. Nobody will walk in on you."

"What's going on in the back room?" asked Marcus.

"Nothing," said Mercy unconvincingly.

Marcus, naturally, peered over the desk at the closed door. "Does anyone else hear croaking?"

I should have known we wouldn't be able to keep our little problem a secret forever.

Daryl stepped up to his side, still clutching the antlers. "I hear it too. Did you order a bunch of frogs for the event? Because Marcus... doesn't like them."

"I most certainly do not," said Marcus.

Wonderful. I bit back a sarcastic comment, instead saying, "They'll be gone by the weekend. If you don't want to go into the hall, you can take the costumes home with you instead."

"What were you planning on doing with them?" Marcus looked between us, suspicion seeping into his expression. "I heard the choir never made it home last night. Is that what happened to them?"

Argh. Why did he have to be so persistent? "There was an accident involving a spell. We're dealing with it, but we didn't expect you to show up this early."

"Someone turned the choir into frogs?" asked Marcus. "Is that what we can expect during our next attempt at a rehearsal?"

"We didn't turn them into frogs on purpose," I said. "Someone put a spell on them, which we're going to reverse as soon as we find a solution."

"It's Janice," added Mercy, who'd apparently given up pretending otherwise. "She's the one playing pranks on us. I'm pretty sure she switched out your costumes too."

"Is that so?" said Marcus. "In that case, then we simply can't take the risk of taking part in your production. I will not have the indignity of being turned into an amphibian. It'll permanently ruin my aspirations of acting in the West End."

Because your ambitions are really the important thing here. "I highly doubt it, Marcus."

Ignoring me, he turned and left the inn. Mercy hastened to run after him, while Daryl hovered in the doorway, wearing an apologetic look. "Sorry about him. We really don't want to be turned into frogs, though."

"You won't be," I said. "Not if we manage to stop Janice, anyway, and I think I know how she's doing this. You know that wishing box you mentioned?"

His brows shot up. "She can't have taken the wishing box."

"It looks like she did," I said. "I wasn't going to tell anyone unless I was certain, but everything that's gone wrong has happened after the box disappeared, and she's at the centre of all of it. If we get the box away from her, there won't be any more issues."

"She can't have taken the wishing box," he repeated. "It's not possible."

"What makes you so sure? How did you even know it was here, anyway?"

A flush swept across his face, but he clammed up when Mercy walked back into the reception area. He'd known we had the box... but had *he* been the one who'd taken it? It made no sense for him to sabotage his own play, but before I could ask him anything else, he muttered an apology and ran out of the inn.

Mercy blinked after him. "What was that about?"

"I told Daryl that Janice is probably using the wishing box to derail our event, but he didn't seem to believe me," I said vaguely. "We have to stop her, though. Otherwise Marcus won't budge, and we can wave farewell to our play."

"Turning the choir back into humans again would be a starting point. It'll be a lot easier to convince the theatre group to come back if they aren't worried about being turned into frogs."

"Yeah, but even if they do turn back, there's still the chance it might happen again. Like the snowstorm. I kept expecting it to come back last night."

"Glad I'm not the only one. I hardly slept at all. I feel

bad for making your parents stay up half the night to work on those antlers too."

"Same here, but I can't sew to save my life," I said. "Besides, Mum and Dad regularly stay up late making hats anyway. This is pretty standard for them."

"Except for the possibility that the antlers will turn into anteaters before the event starts."

"Don't even." I groaned. "Definitely don't mention that to Marcus. In fact, we'll avoid discussing it at all…" I trailed off at the sound of whispering somewhere behind us. "Did you hear that?"

I turned to face the door to the back room, where the croaking had silenced. Instead, unmistakeably human voices drifted out of the room. It seemed the frog spell had worn off at last.

Clearly thinking the same, Mercy ran over to the door and unlocked it, revealing all the choir members huddled together in the back room. Their expressions ranged from confused to sheepish. They also seemed to be missing their clothes. *Oops.*

"Where'd you put the clothes?" I asked Mercy.

"Um… I left them back in the hall," she said. "I'll get them."

Leaving the door closed, we ran into the hall to fetch the piles of clothes and return them to their owners. Naturally, Bella and my parents came walking through the reception area when we were in the middle of handing the first batch of clothes over to the choir, who yelped and tried to hide behind one another when they realised they weren't alone in there.

"What on earth are a bunch of naked people doing in your back room?" asked Bella.

"The choir turned from frogs back into humans again," I said. "I forgot we left their clothes in the hall. They're all free from the spell, though."

"I'm sure that's a welcome consolation for them if they catch their death of cold." She rolled her eyes. "I'm going out."

"Where?" I asked warily.

"Does it matter? Since when were you interested?"

"The person who turned the choir into frogs is still out there. And she has limited chances left to cause more havoc for us before the event begins."

Her brows arched. "You're certain you know who it is?"

"Yes," I said. "The same person Mum and Dad went after yesterday... not that I'm encouraging them to do the same again."

Her gaze flickered over to the half-open door to the back room. "If you say so."

"I'm fairly sure Mum and Dad's antics at Janice's inn are exactly what prompted last night's events," I said. "You won't say anything to encourage them, will you?"

"What do you take me for?" Bella left the inn via the front door, and moments later, the carollers began to file out of the back room. Larry led the way, wearing odd socks and a shirt which was several sizes too big. The others appeared to be in a similar condition, but at least most of them were fully clothed.

"Sorry about the inconvenience," I told them. "You can all go home now. Your families are probably worried about you."

"What about the event this weekend?" asked Larry. "Is the same thing likely to happen again?"

"It was a one-off," Mercy said, but she sounded as unsure as I was. For all we knew, Janice had a whole set of other pranks lined up ready to disrupt the entirety of our event. I didn't blame Larry for looking less than enthused at the possibility of risking his fellow carollers being turned into animals again.

We needed to deal with Janice first.

10

The universe had other ideas. Once the choir had finally dispersed, the guests from the second floor came downstairs to check out, and their replacements arrived in more or less the same moment. An elderly witch and wizard entered the reception area, both dressed in red-and-green ensembles which would have appeared resplendent if they weren't placed next to the attire my parents wore on a daily basis. At least they were easy enough to please, taking a pile of brochures up to their room to arrange their own tours. Nevertheless, as the afternoon wore on, I found myself even more desperate to find time to get our missing wishing box back before Janice decided to send our guests packing on top of wrecking our weekend.

After we'd sent the new guests to their rooms, Mercy tried to call Marcus to tell him we were now frog-free, only to end up getting nothing but a dial tone.

"Not again." She put the phone down. "I swear this thing's broken."

"Or Janice is trying to cover all her bases," I added. "I'm trying to figure out how to prove she's the one who stole the box. It's not like I can sneak in and steal it back without risking getting caught."

Besides, breaking and entering wasn't my thing, even if she'd technically done the same to me when she'd taken it. Unless she'd swiped it from the recycling bin outside, but even that was questionable behaviour. Mercy was the one who'd actually paid for the box, after all.

While Mercy went into the back room to clean up the remnants of the mess the frogs had left behind, the door opened and none other than Janice herself entered the reception area. I stared at her for a moment. "Can I help you?"

"You can start by not spreading rumours about me," she said.

I blinked at her. "What are you talking about?"

"Don't pretend you don't know. I heard from Marcus that you told everyone in the theatre company that I'm the one who stole your costumes. And something about turning people into frogs too."

Oh, no. I'd never considered Marcus might tell tales on us, but if she *was* responsible, now she'd be doubly careful not to give anything away.

"The choir turned into frogs right after the incident with you and my parents," I said. "We have no other suspects, and they wanted an explanation for who was likely to have wanted to cast a spell on them."

Her brows rose. "So you decided to tell everyone I'm the one who did it?"

"I said you were our only suspect. If you can enlighten me on whoever else in town would have a reason to turn our weekend event into a complete fiasco, then I'm all ears."

"You don't need outside interference to turn your own event into a fiasco, Carol. First you can't keep hold of your own reservations, then you have to resort to sending your parents to beg for them back, and now you're accusing me of casting spells on your staff."

That's because it's exactly what you did. And we both know it.

"I don't know, maybe it's because I saw you wandering around here right before everything went to hell?" I said, growing more and more annoyed by the second. "Or because you conveniently decided to start running a similar event only days after ours, tried to hire our choir to work for you when you knew the rehearsals would clash with our event, and stole our catering menu?"

Her face reddened. "You don't own those ideas."

"That doesn't mean you have the right to take supplies we paid for."

"I gave them back!" She was all but shouting now. "What more do you want?"

"No more interference would be nice. What *is* your problem, anyway? We never did anything to you, but I had to give the choir an explanation, and when the same person's name keeps coming up, it's no coincidence."

"Are you joking?" she said. "You're the one who conjured up a storm inside *my* inn. You've done nothing but belittle and challenge me from the moment you opened your doors."

"Speak for yourself." A storm? What on earth was she talking about? I'd never done anything to her at all, in fact, aside from returning her snide comments with my own sarcasm. Even with recent events, the worst I'd done was tell other people my suspicions, because there was only so long I could go on feigning ignorance when I knew perfectly well who wanted our event to fail.

It *must* be her who was responsible.

Before she could say another word, however, my parents walked downstairs and into the reception area. I'd forgotten they were still upstairs, so their reappearance took me off guard. At least they hadn't gone to confront her on Janice's own property this time around, but another standoff between them was the last thing we all needed.

"What are you doing here?" Mum asked her.

Janice glared back. "I could ask you the same question."

"Are you threatening my daughter again?" asked Dad.

"I'm not threatening anyone," Janice said. "I'm telling her to stop spreading lies about me."

"They aren't lies," I said. "I told the theatre group that the reason we had a bunch of frogs locked in the back room is because someone transformed them all at once, and we had one obvious suspect."

"She conjured up a storm inside my inn," said Janice, "but you don't see me telling the entire town about it."

"That's because I didn't do it."

She scoffed. "Then how do you explain the floods in my basement?"

"I have no idea what you're talking about," I said. "Maybe someone left a tap running."

"Hilarious. I suppose you thought it was funny to make bells jingle above my bed at all hours of the morning too."

"Um… what?" I asked.

Both my parents looked at me in a confusion which matched my own. What in the world was she trying to accuse me of? The idea of jingling bells hanging above her bed was an amusing one, I'd admit, but not something I'd have wasted my time inflicting on her when I had enough to occupy my attention. Had she resorted to making up downright fiction to justify her attempts to undercut Mercy and me at every turn?

"I didn't do anything," I said. "How could I? I've been run off my feet all week. Besides, I wouldn't waste my time with anything so petty."

"Then why are you so quick to assume I'd do the same?" Janice asked.

"Because this all started when a wishing box Mercy and I ordered for our event went missing, which incidentally was right after I ran into you outside the inn. If you can prove you didn't take it, I'll gladly apologise and set the record straight."

"I can't have taken it," she said, "because I didn't even know you were having a wishing box delivered."

"Neither did I before it showed up," I said. "Besides, my mother's familiar hid it around the back of the inn, in the recycling bin. Anyone might have taken it."

"I'm allergic to cats," she said.

"Would that stop you from picking up something that would make every wish you made come true for as long as it remained in your possession?"

Her mouth pressed together. "I didn't take it."

I'd have called her a liar, but her comments about me flooding her basement had caught me off guard. Not to mention the jingling bells. "There can't be someone else setting us against one another, can there?"

"No way," she said. "You started it."

"I really didn't. Can you think of anyone who might have anything to gain from using the wishing box against both of us at once?"

"You tell me that. It sounds like you're making excuses to me."

"I didn't even know you thought I'd done anything to you until a minute ago," I pointed out. "You *did* start planning your event right after ours and buy all the reindeer costumes in town. You can't deny that."

"I didn't steal anything from you," she protested.

"Except for our catering order." Her wide-eyed innocence had almost sounded convincing, but if she kept denying what I'd witnessed with my own eyes, how could I trust a word she said? "Look, I don't want to argue with you all day. How about we both agree to leave one another alone? If you don't touch my event, I won't touch yours."

Never mind that I'd had no intention of going near *her* event to begin with, but if she assumed that I'd stoop to the same level as her, maybe this was the only way to get her to agree to leave us alone for the time being.

"Fine." She looked as though she wanted to say more, but with my parents staring her down, she was outnumbered. Without another word, she turned and left the inn, the door swinging shut behind her.

"That was interesting," said Dad. "She seemed awfully certain of her innocence."

"Yes, but it was probably an act," I said. "I didn't do anything to her at all. If someone *is* messing with her, it's definitely not me."

Mercy returned to the reception area, a mop in her

hands from where she'd been cleaning up the mess the frogs had left behind. "What on earth is going on?"

"Janice," I said. "Sounds like the theatre group told her I claimed she was the one who turned the choir into frogs."

"Seriously?" she asked. "Let me guess… she denied it all."

"You've got it." Yet it seemed odd that she'd been hit by an apparent prankster too. Unless she was lying or exaggerating, of course, but why would she admit to being humiliated in that way? I wouldn't have expected her to confess to me of all people that someone had set up a bunch of jingling bells above her bed. Granted, I'd confessed to her about the frog incident and the rabbit costumes, but only because I'd been certain she'd been behind all our misfortune. And I still thought so, despite her attempts to claim otherwise.

Mercy's brow scrunched up. "So she came here to yell at you… why?"

"Because she thinks I flooded her basement, conjured up a storm, and unleashed jingling bells above her bed, apparently." I shook my head. "I think she was talking complete nonsense, personally. Maybe she's finally cracked. Or someone targeted both of us in order to make us blame one another, but she categorically dismissed that as a possibility."

Her eyes widened. "What, someone's using the wishing box to set us against one another?"

"It's not like they needed much encouragement, did they?"

Our rivalry was well-known, but who on earth would be vindictive enough to target both of us at once? Unless

Janice had managed to make herself another enemy. It wasn't that implausible, given her general attitude towards anyone she perceived to be her rival, but why they'd go after Mercy and me as well was a mystery.

If someone *was* trying to set us against one another, they wouldn't have had to try very hard. But where did that leave the wishing box… and if Janice didn't have it, who did?

11

Since Janice had left us with more questions than answers and no conclusive proof of her involvement in the frog incident *or* the theft of the wishing box, we had nothing to do but return to our preparations for the weekend's event while crossing our fingers that she'd stick to her promise to stay out of it. To start off with, the choir of frogs had left the back room covered in random discarded articles of clothing which needed to be dealt with once Mercy had finished mopping the floor.

"Who went home without shoes?" I asked. "Or socks?"

"Probably the same person who left their underwear behind." Mercy wrinkled her nose, dropping a pile of clothes behind the counter. "We'll put it all in lost and found for the choir to pick up later."

"Wise idea." We had yet to get through to the theatre company on the phone, but at least if they came back here with an update on the costumes, we'd be able to prove their changing room was now frog-free. Then, provided

Janice kept her word and didn't interfere, the show might go on after all.

I can't believe she accused me of casting spells on her inn. Okay, I'd thought the same of her, but at least I had something resembling proof. This whole situation was giving me a headache, frankly, and reasoning with Janice was as futile as having a shouting match with one of my parents' hats.

Mercy picked up the phone and called the costume shop—again—while I lined up the antlers my parents had made for the theatre group in a fit of hopeful optimism. Pairing the antlers with the rabbit costumes kept me occupied until Mercy hung up the phone in triumph.

"That's the costume situation officially dealt with," she said. "I cancelled our request at the local shop and then told the online shop that we'll stick with what we have. I highly doubt the audience will guess our reindeer used to be rabbits."

"Definitely not." I held up one of the costumes in demonstration. "Have you heard from the choir yet about how they're coping after their overnight ordeal?"

"No, but Marcus finally texted me. I think he's coming back to talk to us again."

"Then we'd better hope it's good news. I don't blame him for worrying about being turned into a frog, but we have less than two days until the event. There's no time for us to find replacements for the entire cast. Besides, there's absolutely nothing wrong with the costumes."

"No, there isn't." Regardless, she began nervously pacing as we waited for Marcus to show up. After she'd gone to mop the back room for the fifth time, the door opened and Marcus entered the inn, the costume we'd loaned to Daryl to try on draped over his arm.

"The costume was okay, wasn't it?" I asked him.

"The costume is fine," said Marcus, "but I ran into Janice again on my way here, and she had yet more stories about you blaming her for your misfortune this week."

I stifled a groan. *Again?* I hadn't thought she and Marcus had even been on speaking terms before she'd taken to telling tales on me to him. "She marched in here half an hour ago and yelled accusations at me. Did she mention that part?"

"From her viewpoint, you are the one who levelled accusations at her," he said. "Which frankly leaves me sceptical as to whether you were telling the entire truth about the situation with your unfortunate choir."

"I told the truth as I knew it." I tried to keep my tone calm. I really did. "She's been making nonstop attempts to sabotage our event this weekend, but we've come to a truce and promised no more interference on either side. Regardless of whether or not she was responsible for the incident with the choir and the frogs, there will be no repeat performance."

"Good. I hope that this ridiculous matter is behind us. In the meantime, I'd like to do one last rehearsal, in costume this time."

"What—you mean now?" I glanced at Mercy, disarmed. "Not all the costumes are ready yet, but if you don't mind that, then we can have the hall ready for you in a couple of hours."

"Fine," he said. "I expect the costumes all to be ready and in perfect condition by the weekend."

I suppressed the impulse to tell him my own parents

were making the costumes and we weren't getting paid any extra for it, but it wouldn't be a good idea to tick him off at this point. Not when we were so close to getting the event back on track.

"They will be," I said.

He left the inn while a flutter of hope stirred inside me at the notion that maybe we had the slightest chance of salvaging the weekend after all. As long as the rehearsal went through without a hitch, of course.

"Wow," said Mercy. "Guess I should check the hall for any potential sources of trouble."

"Or the wishing box," I added. "In case it's shown up again. Wouldn't be the strangest thing that's happened this week."

"You've got that right." Mercy entered the hall while I checked every single costume so Marcus would have absolutely nothing to complain about.

Bella returned not long afterwards, watching in confusion as I paired each rabbit costume with one of the handmade sets of antlers.

"What's going on?" she asked.

"The theatre group is coming back soon for another rehearsal." I picked up the next rabbit costume and carefully tucked the ears inside the hood to hide them.

My sister groaned. "Why do you need another one?"

"Because we didn't have any costumes the first time around. Anyway, this time it's the theatre group, not the choir."

"That's just as bad." She retreated up the stairs, saying over her shoulder, "It wouldn't kill you to invest in soundproofed walls, you know."

"Only if you're willing to pay for them," I said after

WINTER WISHES

her. "Also, you do realise you'll have to sit through the whole thing again tomorrow, don't you?"

My sister didn't look back. *Ah, well. It's not like she wasn't forewarned.*

A few hours later, the theatre group showed up with their usual flair and enthusiasm. Most were thrilled the performance was back on, except Marcus, and he never appeared to be enthusiastic about anything. He could win an Oscar and take the prize with the exact same expression of dead seriousness. Still, the others made up for his lack of festive spirit, exclaiming delightedly over the reindeer costumes my parents had pulled together. Marcus insisted on sending the others into the back room first to make sure there were no frogs or spells lurking around before he went in there himself, but not one single amphibian made an appearance. Better still, nobody raised any objections to our idea of combining the rabbit costumes with the new antlers my parents had put together.

Once everyone was in costume, the dress rehearsal kicked off. Even though we'd seen the play a dozen times before, the group's mood was infectious despite the lack of an actual audience. The reindeer cavorted across the stage, circling around Marcus as he raised his antler-clad head to deliver his line.

A shout rang out from the wings, followed by another. Marcus ignored the noise and continued with his line, but the screams rose louder, drowning out his voice. His jaw twitched with annoyance, but he was too good an actor to let an inexplicable noise put him off his game. The others, though, kept looking around for the source of the noise, completely distracted.

Mercy grabbed my arm and pointed at the stage with a horrified expression. "The tinsel is moving."

I followed her gaze to the tinsel looped around the walls, silver and green and red, which moved as though in a faint breeze. The tinsel circling the edges of the stage was in a similar state, slithering across the ground. Wait, *slithering?*

"What the—?"

One of the pieces of tinsel detached itself and raised its head to look up at the actors onstage, a hissing noise escaping it.

Snakes. All the tinsel draped around the stage had turned into live snakes. Heads arose from among the glittering loops, baring sharp teeth at the actors, who stood frozen on the stage in dawning horror as they realised they were surrounded by angry serpents. From the distant screams from the wings, they'd run into trouble, too, but before we could run in and help, a tinsel-snake became detached from the wall and flopped onto the floor. Then another landed beside it. Needless to say, the snakes weren't thrilled to hit the ground from a sudden fall. More hissing ensued, followed by a strangled yelp from Mercy as a snake detached itself from the row of chairs behind us and slithered away to freedom.

"Get away from our stage!" Marcus bellowed at the nearest snake, reindeer antlers bobbing on his head. He then recoiled when the snake bared its tiny fangs at him.

"Don't provoke them!" I warned. "Everyone, stay on the stage! We'll get rid of them."

"Hang on," Mercy said. "I'd better make sure there aren't any others loose in the inn."

"Go ahead." Thanking the universe that we'd opted

against putting tinsel inside the guests' rooms, I watched her run towards the reception area, exclaiming in horror as she opened the door to reveal the vibrant tree next to the desk. *Even the tinsel on the tree is alive.* "Someone needs to turn off the lights."

The snakes might not have existed until a few minutes ago, but that didn't mean we needed to traumatise everyone by accidentally electrocuting them with the Christmas tree lights.

"I'll do it." Mercy ran out of the hall, letting the door close behind her, while I did my best to calm down the panicking theatre group.

"Don't move or you might tread on one of them," I said to them. "Just stay calm and still. No, you can't leave the hall. There are snakes out there too."

In fact, I strongly suspected every single piece of tinsel in the entire inn had turned into a live snake. It was the blizzard incident all over again—except worse. The actors were too busy panicking to pay any attention to my commands to stay out of range of the snakes, which were having the time of their short lives slithering around the rows of empty seats. Glad at our lack of an audience, I whirled on the stage when I heard a strangled yell.

"It bit me!" Daryl, typically, had fallen off the stage and landed straight beside a snake's waiting fangs. The snake itself made a break for it as I ran to his side.

Oh, no. I looked up at the stage. "Does anyone know if those snakes are venomous?"

"How would I know?" someone asked. "I've never seen one before."

Right. Snakes weren't exactly a common sight at the

North Pole. Heart sinking even further, I grabbed my phone from my pocket. "I'll call the hospital."

Nobody else volunteered, instead simply staring gormlessly while Daryl lay moaning on the floor. Panic gripped me like a vice as I called an ambulance, crossing my fingers behind my back that the bite *wasn't* deadly. I wouldn't have thought a magically conjured snake would be able to kill anyone with deadly venom, but how could anyone know for sure? Most people here hadn't seen a snake before, much less one which had been tinsel until recently.

The door opened, and Mercy came running over to Daryl's side, hopping over several more snakes on her journey across the hall. "Daryl! Are you okay?"

Even in his current state, Daryl still blushed at Mercy's attention. "One of the snakes bit me."

"I'm so sorry!" she exclaimed. "Don't move. Carol—"

"I called an ambulance," I said. "They'll be here soon. A snake that's not actually real can't be venomous, right?"

"Uh." Mercy's gaze dropped to Daryl's prone form. "I don't know. The doctors will sort you out, though."

Daryl moaned faintly. "Mercy… I wanted to tell you you're beautiful. Before I die."

"You aren't dying," she said, her face equally red. "Just hang in there while we clear the way for the doctors to get in."

"Good idea." The last thing we needed was for the snakes to attack the emergency services when they showed up, so we'd have to find a way to herd them somewhere they couldn't bite anyone. With the theatre group stranded on the stage and surrounded by a sea of snakes, it seemed a tall order.

Mercy blew out a breath. "Okay... I have no idea if this is going to work or not. Fair warning."

"What are you—?" I broke off as she raised a hand and several snowflakes drifted down from the ceiling onto the wriggling snakes below.

They didn't like that. Not a bit. Hissing, they squirmed out of the way of the growing snowstorm while Mercy directed the snowflakes to herd them across the hall. Improvising, I hopped across a row of chairs until I reached a snake-free part of the hall. Then I turned several chairs over and moved them into a circle, forming a kind of cage, and beckoned to Mercy to drive the snakes in that direction.

The tide of glittering snakes headed towards the cage, dodging snowflakes on the way, but it was slow going. Thankfully, a couple of brave theatre group members picked up brooms and other props to help us nudge our reptilian guests across the room, though Marcus was not among them. Before we'd finished, the emergency services showed up. Mercy took a quick break to make sure they had Daryl safely removed from the hall, while I continued to herd snakes into our improvised cage.

Two doctors carted Daryl away, loading him onto the sleigh which served as an ambulance, after which Mercy returned to help me out.

"He'll be fine," said Mercy. "I'm sure he will. You're right... it's not a real snake, is it?"

"Looks pretty real to me." I glanced over at Marcus, who glared daggers at me, and instantly regretted making eye contact. "Let's get the rest of them into the cage before anyone else gets bitten."

By now, most of the snakes had entered our improvised cage, where they had plenty of space to wriggle around. The theatre group, meanwhile, took the opportunity to make an escape into the reception area as we herded the last of the snakes into our trap.

After pushing the last chair into place, we checked for gaps in our improvised cage. We'd have to leave our unwanted wildlife inside the cage until the spell wore off because there was no chance that I'd risk any of them escaping by moving them to the dressing room again. Besides, this time they wouldn't turn back into humans.

"I hope Daryl is okay." Mercy watched the pile of snakes wriggle around their cage. "He… I can't believe he said that to me. I didn't know he liked me in that way."

"I think it's safe to say *he* never had the wishing box," I said.

"Why?" Comprehension dawned on her face. "Did he mention liking me? He told you?"

"He did. I thought you'd rather hear it from him, so I didn't say anything. You don't mind, do you?"

"No… I don't think I do," she said, sounding thoughtful. "I never thought of him in that way. He was very sweet."

"Yeah, he was. He… well, he admitted he wanted to use the box to give him the courage to ask you out. I told him I wasn't sure the box's magic would do that for him."

"He wanted to use the box?" she echoed.

"Yes, but I'm pretty sure that same wish wouldn't have made all the tinsel turn into snakes. I don't think he used it."

"No… I doubt it." Her gaze drifted over to the snakes' cage. "Janice… so much for her promise, huh."

"I know." For all that, though, we couldn't prove Janice

was the person responsible. Not as long as she remained in a stubborn attitude of denial. "Okay… we need to deal with the theatre group."

In the reception area, the disgruntled actors had gathered, most of them still in costume. My heart swooped down to my shoes as Marcus faced me with a glare that would put a venomous snake to shame.

"You can keep the costumes," he said. "We won't be acting in your play this weekend."

"I…" I had no counterargument. "The snakes will be gone by tomorrow."

"And so will we," he said. "Come on, everyone."

My last hope went out like the final ember of a fire as he and the others departed. A couple of them gave me apologetic looks, but none of them stayed back and offered us any words of comfort.

"Who would have wanted this?" whispered Mercy.

"Janice did it." My eyes stung. "She must have."

But the others no longer believed me. Nobody did, except for Mercy.

12

After the theatre group's departure, Mercy and I took five minutes to mope and then moved to planning what to do next. While I wanted to go and confront Janice face-to-face at once, we needed to figure out how to refund everyone's tickets for the play or else think of an alternative form of entertainment for the weekend. Assuming anyone still turned up, which would likely depend on how soon we could get rid of our reptilian visitors currently wriggling around the hall.

There was also the choir to think of, who'd already spent all this time putting together their performance schedule for the weekend. The idea of letting them down with no explanation didn't sit right with me. On the other hand, every sudden movement set my nerves on edge, and I kept thinking I saw snakes lurking in every shadow as I searched for any stray bits of tinsel we might have overlooked. It was lucky the guests had all gone out for the day—with the exception of Bella—but they'd be back for the evening meal soon enough, and it wouldn't surprise me if they all packed up and left on the spot.

"We have to tell the guests there's a bunch of snakes loose in here," Mercy said, as if sensing my thoughts. "Not to mention the kitchen staff."

"I have to tell my family too." I suppressed a groan. "I suppose it'll stop them from spending the night making more sets of antlers, at least."

Which was no consolation whatsoever. We'd lost while Janice had won, and we hadn't been able to do anything to stop her.

"I'll tell the kitchen staff, then," she said. "Can you handle the guests?"

"Sure." Since the one guest present was Bella, I resigned myself to dealing with her attitude turned up to the max when she found out what'd gone wrong this time.

Bracing myself, I went upstairs and knocked on the door to my family's suite.

"What?" came Bella's muffled voice from inside.

"It's me," I said.

She pulled the door open a moment later. "Thought Mum and Dad had lost their keys again."

"Nah, they still aren't back yet." My chest tightened at the sight of their half-sewn reindeer antlers littering the room. They'd done their best to pull the replacement costumes together for me, and Janice had screwed it all up anyway. Had I really expected her to be visited by three cranky ghosts in the middle of the night and have a change of heart? I should have known better.

"What's up?" she asked. "Did Charlie kill one of your frogs?"

"What—no. The frogs are now human again. The bad news is that our tinsel is now snakes."

"You're joking." She sprang across the room to Mum and Dad's teetering piles of souvenirs, warily peering into the bag of decorations they'd bought. "That looks normal. Check it out."

I strode to her side and eyed the bag of tinsel. Not remotely snake-like. "Maybe the spell only targeted the decorations hanging on the walls. I'd tell Mum and Dad not to hang it up until the spell wears off."

"Not to hang what up?" Mum pushed open the door and bustled into the room, wielding yet another handful of souvenir bags. Dad sauntered in behind her, his cheeks flushed with the cold and a towering gift-box-shaped hat perched precariously on his head.

"Tinsel," I said, defeated. "You didn't see Mercy on the way in?"

"No," she said. "Need more costumes?"

Mercy must still be dealing with the kitchen staff, then. I stepped away from the bag and looked between my parents. "No. By the way, don't go into the hall downstairs. There are snakes on the loose."

"Snakes?" asked Dad.

"Yeah, someone turned our tinsel into snakes," I explained. "Just a temporary spell, I think, but I don't want any of you to get bitten."

Bella's gaze flickered to my face. "You're serious? All the tinsel downstairs is now snakes?"

"Yes, and the theatre group is now minus one member," I said.

Bella's face went ashen. "What does that mean?"

"It means he got bitten." I leaned wearily against Mum

and Dad's hat-covered bed. "He's in the hospital. I'd rather none of you ends up joining him, so please avoid the hall until the spell is undone."

"We won't go into the hall, don't worry," Mum said. "Carolyn, are you okay?"

"No, my weekend is collapsing around my ears." I left the room before I started a Bella-style life-is-unfair whine, and Charlie brushed against my ankles. "Mum, your familiar is out here. Tell him not to go into the hall, either."

Mum moved in to coax her familiar into the room, while the echoing sound of a door slamming came from downstairs.

"What now?" I ran for the stairs, pausing to check for snakes before climbing down to the reception area.

Mercy stared forlornly at the door. "The kitchen staff took off. Said the place was a hazard."

"Great." I pressed a hand to my forehead. "Just what we need."

"Not permanently," she added. "Only until the snakes are gone. I didn't have the chance to break it to them that we aren't going ahead with the event yet, but I imagine they've probably guessed by now."

"They'll have to eat all the snacks by themselves. Or we'll give them to the guests, assuming they want to stick around."

Mercy moved back behind the desk. "Guess I should call the choir and tell them the bad news."

"I'll have to stick a warning sign on the door to the hall too," I said. "Most of the guests aren't in at the moment, and we don't want any of them wandering in there before the spell wears off."

"Good point. I take it your parents weren't fazed?"

"Not in the slightest." I rolled my eyes at the ceiling. "Okay, I'll put a sign on the door while you contact the choir."

"Deal." She picked up the phone while I repurposed an abandoned banner to say 'Beware Snakes' and stuck it across the door to the hall. Not my finest work, but it'd do the job.

Now to deal with another pressing matter.

Mercy put down the phone. "I can't get through to them. Where are you going?"

I grabbed my coat. "I'm going to Janice's place to get the wishing box back. I know I said I wouldn't, but Janice broke our agreement within a couple of hours of us making it. I'm sick of taking the high road while she walks all over us."

"So you're going to steal the box back by yourself?" asked Mercy. "Want backup?"

"Nah, you should keep an eye on things here. Besides, if I get caught, one of us needs to be able to keep the inn running."

Besides, this was personal. While confronting Janice alone was probably a bad idea, I had nothing to lose at this point.

I needed to get that box back.

A loud meow drew my attention to Charlie the familiar, who'd somehow slipped downstairs again. "You're supposed to be in my parents' room. There's snakes on the loose down here."

I picked him up to take him back upstairs, but he wriggled out of my grip and meowed loudly.

"Don't you start," I told him. "I have something important I need to do."

A second loud meow startled me, especially when he then circled my legs and started to nudge me towards the door. "You want to come with me to see Janice? Really?"

I couldn't exactly communicate with him the way Mum could, but I was beginning to wonder if he understood something of what was going on in here after all.

"Can he understand you?" asked Mercy.

The cat meowed in reply.

"He understands my mum," I said. "I'll ask her."

I dodged Charlie's attempts to herd me out the door and instead coaxed him upstairs, where I knocked on the door to my family's room. "Charlie followed me downstairs."

"Oh." Mum opened the door. "Come back in, Charlie."

"I think he wants to come with me," I said. "To look for the missing wishing box. He hid it outside in his hiding spot a few days ago, so there's a chance he might be able to help me find it."

"He hid it?"

"Yeah, before it vanished. Would he be able to recognise it if he saw it again?"

"Yes, I think he would." Mum crouched beside her familiar and spoke to him. "If you're sure you want to go and look for it, then you can take him with you."

"Thanks." It was a long shot, but if Janice had hidden the box, Charlie ought to be able to seek it out without me having to sneak into all the rooms at her inn myself. I still ran the risk of one of us getting caught in the act, of course, but that way I wouldn't have to do the stealth part myself.

With Charlie in my arms—he refused to walk in the snow—I walked swiftly down the road and towards Janice's inn, hardly pausing for breath. Anger spurred me on, coupled with a fair bit of despair. I couldn't believe Janice had gone so far as to risk someone dying of a snake bite for the sake of revenge, especially after she and I had agreed to leave one another alone, but that's what I got for assuming there were depths to which she wouldn't sink. Granted, the way the wishing box operated wasn't necessarily within the user's control, but Janice ought to have known from the frog and blizzard incidents that the situation could easily spiral beyond her intentions, and she'd still used the box again.

Before I entered Janice's inn, I set Charlie down on the doorstep. "I'm pretty sure the box is somewhere in there. Can you bring it outside and meet me at the corner over there?"

The cat shook his head irritably, as though unimpressed at the notion of having to walk through the snow to our meeting point, but it was that or risk getting caught on the doorstep. Hoping he understood me, I left him to sneak in via the back door and entered the lobby myself.

Janice scowled at me over the desk. "What now?"

"Are you serious?" I folded my arms across my chest. "I should never have expected you to keep your word, but getting someone hospitalised is too much even for you."

She blinked. "I'm sorry, what?"

"The snakes," I said. "One of the theatre group members is in the hospital, our guests have all been placed in danger, and our event's cancelled. Are you happy now?"

"You're out of your mind. I didn't put anyone in the hospital."

"You may as well have," I said. "Did you even read the instructions on that box before you started using it to try to sabotage us?"

"You know what I think? I think you sabotaged your own event and then blamed it on me. I suppose you thought it'd be good publicity."

"Seriously?" I arched a brow. "That's what you're going with?"

"It's no more implausible than the alternative. I've had enough of being accused of things I didn't do."

"You're the only person who'd have had reason to wreck our weekend," I said. "Besides, you took the wishing box."

"I don't have your missing box. Get out of here or I'm calling the police."

I very nearly dared her to do exactly that, but Charlie was still elsewhere in the inn, looking for the box. Once I had it back in hand, it didn't matter if she denied all my accusations. I'd be able to get myself out of this situation without needing to worry about her any longer.

"Fine," I said. "But I'm not taking your word for it the next time you make any promises."

Hoping she wouldn't guess I'd sent Mum's familiar to sneak around the rooms, I left for our meetup point on the corner, walking as slowly as I dared while I waited for the cat to catch me up.

My heart leapt when I finally spotted him padding towards me then sank just as fast when it immediately became apparent that he wasn't carrying the wishing box.

I crouched beside the little cat as he approached me and sprang into my arms. "Didn't you find the wishing box?"

Oh, no. It seemed Janice hadn't lied when she'd said she didn't have the box. That didn't mean she hadn't previously had it in her possession, but I hadn't considered the possibility that she'd get rid of the evidence. Maybe she'd given it to someone else for safekeeping, but who might that be?

For now, I carried Charlie back to the inn and found Mercy on the phone again. She hung up as I released the cat, who shook off the bits of snow which had landed on his ears and padded upstairs without looking back.

"Daryl is fine," she said. "Turns out the bite wasn't deadly. Did you get the box?"

"Janice doesn't have it," I said. "She's still claiming I'm making up the whole thing, and Charlie went looking for the box and didn't find it anywhere on her property."

"Seriously? How is that possible?"

"I have no idea. I thought she might have given it away to someone else, but it's not like I know who she'd have trusted to look after something so valuable."

"Nor me. Does she even have any friends?"

"Haven't a clue," I said. "Have the other guests come back yet?"

"No, and we're going to have to come up with an alternative dinner menu now we have no kitchen staff."

I'd forgotten that slight issue. "We do have a bunch of unused snacks for the weekend..."

"You want to serve our guests snowflake cakes and reindeer cookies?"

"Do you have a better idea?" I rubbed my forehead. "It's that or order a takeaway delivery. The guests might appreciate the variety, I guess."

"Yeah... we might as well do something with the buffet snacks, though."

She didn't add what we were both thinking: that surrendering the snacks would mean admitting the event was doomed. Despite it all, a sliver of hope remained; if I could just figure out who *did* have the wishing box, then we might be able to snatch victory from the jaws of defeat after all. "I was so certain Janice took the box. Am I losing my mind?"

"Probably." Bella entered the reception area.

I frowned at her. "What are you doing downstairs? I told you to stay in your room."

"Technically, you only told Mum and Dad to stay in the room," she said. "They're going overboard making new costumes again."

"Why? We don't need them anymore now the event is cancelled."

Her brows rose. "You cancelled it?"

"Not officially, but we can't exactly get on with the show with no theatre group and a bunch of snakes locked in our hall."

"I thought you said they were going to turn back into tinsel soon."

"They are," said Mercy, "but Marcus and the others don't want to risk it happening again during the final performance."

"Oh," said my sister. "I'm sorry."

She sounded almost... contrite. Which was weird, and possibly a first in my lifetime.

I shook my head. "Never mind. I'll talk to Mum and Dad about alternative uses for their costumes."

Maybe they could sell custom antlers in their hat

store. That way, at least one of us would get something positive out of this mess.

I trailed upstairs and found Charlie the cat nudging open the door to my family's room.

"Carolyn!" said Mum as I caught the door before it closed. "How'd it go?"

"Not great," I said. "Charlie couldn't find the wishing box. Either Janice wasn't responsible at all, or she got rid of the box before we could get our hands on it."

"Oh, no," she said. "Should we go and talk to her, then?"

"Don't. We've done all we can. If I push her any further, she'll have us arrested. There's no evidence against her. If someone else has the box, I can't figure out who it is."

Dad moved a pile of antlers across the bed. "Are you sure there's nothing we can do?"

"There really isn't. You don't need to keep making the costumes, either."

"But we're having fun with it," said Mum. "We should have started making holiday-themed hats sooner."

"You can always sell them in your shop, then. Take them home with you."

"Unless you wanted to sell them here at the inn, to make up for the lost ticket sales?" Dad suggested. "We can't fly them all home with us."

I blinked at him. "That's not a bad idea, but are you sure? I mean, you're the ones who made them."

"It's no problem," said Mum. "Most places don't ship to the North Pole, I heard."

"You aren't wrong," I said, surprised at their relative

thoughtfulness. "Might make up for Janice buying every reindeer costume in town."

"Exactly," Mum said. "Want to help us out?"

Normally I'd have refused, but I figured I might as well do something useful rather than sitting around moping. I could've tried to cook dinner, of course, but given how the week had been going so far, I wouldn't have been surprised if I accidentally started a fire. No, we'd be better off ordering something from one of the local takeaway shops instead. "Sure, I'll help for a bit."

I started by moving the stack of antlers to a corner of the room to free up some space on the bed. Doing something useful did help my mood a little, though it wasn't like my week could get any worse. I needed to check with Mercy about pricing, but I could've done worse than hide among a pile of antlers to avoid my problems. Better than picking another fight with Janice.

As I moved over to Bella's side of the room, I found a piece of paper lying on the floor. Frowning, I picked it up. Scrawled across it in my sister's handwriting were the words *I wish the rehearsal would stop.*

I stared at the note, disbelief filtering through. Bella had made a wish, written it down... and the rehearsal *had* stopped. Because the tinsel had turned into snakes and stopped our entire event in its tracks.

"Sweetheart, what's that?" asked Mum.

"It was Bella," I said. "She wrote this."

I showed both of them the note, which they stared at in silence for several seconds. Then we all turned in unison as the door opened and Bella herself entered the room.

"What?" she asked. "What are you looking at?"

I held up the note. "Did you write this?"

"What is it?" She walked closer then froze mid-step as her gaze took in her own handwriting on the page.

I lowered my hand. "You wanted the rehearsal to stop."

"Of course I did," she said. "I hated that noise."

"Someone got bitten by a snake which might have been deadly." I clenched my hand over the note. "Janice is out to get me because I accused her of using the wishing box to sabotage our event. But—are you saying it was you the whole time?"

"Hang on a second," she said. "I wasn't saying I did anything."

"Why else would you write it down?"

She ducked her head, a flush spreading across her cheeks. "That isn't what it looks like."

"It looks like you wanted to ruin our rehearsal, which is exactly how it turned out," I said. "Now our plans are in tatters. All of them."

Her mouth opened and closed like a goldfish. "I didn't do it."

"You wrote this note."

She didn't say a word in her own defence, simply turning around and leaving the room. Meanwhile, Mum and Dad both watched me with such sad expressions that I wished the floor would swallow me up.

"I don't think she did it," Mum said. "She wouldn't have ruined your plans."

"Why did she write this note, then?" I threw it down on the floor. "Is the box in here?"

"The wishing box?" she asked. "I haven't seen it."

"Nor have I," said Dad. "I don't think she's taken that

note outside of the room, either. I saw her writing in a notepad earlier."

"If the wishing box was in here," Mum said, "then Charlie would have found it."

Her familiar meowed as though in agreement. He hadn't found it in Janice's inn, either, but it made no sense for Bella to act as if the box was in her possession if it was nowhere in sight.

"Then what was the point of her writing the note?"

"Maybe she just wanted to write down her feelings on paper," Dad suggested.

She hadn't put the note in the wishing box, then? That didn't erase her intentions, but the only way to know for sure was to confirm the box wasn't in the room.

I crouched and peered under Bella's bed and then into her suitcase. Guilt jabbed icy fingers into me as I sifted through her clothes, made worse by my parents' silent onlooking. Yet no matter how hard I searched, no signs of the box materialised on her side of the room.

My gaze went to the piles of hats surrounding my parents' bed and the towering stacks of souvenirs.

"You can search, if you like." Mum stood.

I didn't move. "Are you absolutely sure she never took the note out of the room?"

"She didn't," Mum said. "She might have written it on the first night."

"During the first rehearsal?" I asked.

Dad nodded. "Yes, I remember seeing her writing in a notebook then. It makes sense that she was annoyed at first, but she didn't write anything during the more recent rehearsal."

"But…" I faltered. "She hates it here."

"I think it's growing on her," Mum said. "She told me."

"She didn't tell *me* that." A fresh wave of guilt swirled inside me. "She said she came here to make sure both of you didn't get into trouble, nothing more."

"I know," said Mum. "She hates snow, poor thing, but she wanted to see you for the first time in months."

"She didn't mention that either." Not that either of us was great at being honest with one another. Besides, she'd wanted the rehearsal to stop and had gone as far as to write it down with the intention of putting it in the wishing box—which she'd definitely seen on her first day, before it'd disappeared. How was I to know for sure that she hadn't got her hands on it at any point?

I'd already searched the room, though, confirming that Bella didn't have the wishing box in her possession. Now my sister wasn't talking to me on top of everything else. And I hadn't the faintest idea how to fix any of this.

13

After leaving my parents' room, I went downstairs and found Mercy alone in the reception area. "Did you see Bella?"

"She just went out," Mercy said. "Is she okay? She seemed pretty upset."

My chest tightened. "I may have accused her of stealing the wishing box herself."

"You didn't... did you?"

"She had a wish written down on a piece of paper," I explained. "It said she wanted the rehearsal to stop, in no uncertain terms."

Her mouth opened. "Oh."

"Exactly," I said. "Mum and Dad are proclaiming her innocence, but with Janice off the hook, I have no idea who else would want to sabotage our event."

She sucked in a breath. "Is there a way to get your sister to admit the truth? It's got to be easier than dealing with Janice."

"Maybe. Mum and Dad think she wrote the note the

first night and never put it in the box. I looked all over their room and didn't find any signs of it, either."

She grimaced. "To be honest, it sounds like she just got unlucky when she left the note lying around and didn't have the box after all. Unless there's another hiding place we don't know about."

"But our rehearsal *did* get wrecked. In style." I indicated the door to the hall, from behind which a series of hissing noises issued. "Though I don't think she'd have wanted *that* to be the result."

"No, I wouldn't have thought so," said Mercy. "All right. We need to redo the dinner menu before the other guests get back."

We spent the rest of the evening brainstorming alternative plans for the weekend, none of which amounted to anything, and trying not to look at the almost sold-out tickets to the play without any plans for how to refund them. When the other guests showed up after their tour, they assumed the snakes were part of some secret plan for the weekend. I hadn't the heart to tell them otherwise, nor that our last-minute menu change wasn't due to the kitchen staff being occupied with preparations for the event. While my parents were as unbothered as ever, Bella didn't return as the evening passed, and I started to worry that she'd stay out all night.

In the end, I could only do so much wallowing before I wanted to start fixing the damage, even if it was too late to salvage the actual event. While Mercy went to bed early, I ended up pacing around the lower floor in the dark, waiting for Bella to get back so I could apologise to her in person.

My sister didn't return until nearly midnight. I'd

nearly tripped over Charlie four times before the door opened and Bella walked into the reception area. The instant she saw me, she backed straight out of the door.

"Don't leave," I said. "I'm sorry. That's all I wanted to say."

She shrugged but otherwise didn't move. "Does that mean you believe I didn't ruin your rehearsal?"

"I don't think you'd willingly set a bunch of snakes loose on everyone," I said. "So… yes. I believe you."

"You're welcome to tell the theatre group I'm the one responsible," she said. "If that makes them come back."

I frowned. "But… you didn't, right?"

"Does it matter?" She closed the door firmly behind her, as though to avoid looking me in the eyes. "You're losing all your hard work one way or another, and if you can't find the real culprit, then you might as well blame me."

"But…" I trailed off when she turned back around, and I glimpsed the sheen of tears in her eyes. "I don't want you to take the heat for something you didn't do."

"Some heat would be nice right now," she said in a half-hearted attempt at humour.

"Look, I'm sorry. I found the note in your handwriting, and…"

"And you were upset, I get it. Look, I'll be going home in a few days. I don't mind if you tell them I did it."

"I do." I meant it too. "I know I screwed up."

"It's up to you." She climbed the stairs back to her room, leaving me feeling worse than ever. Blinking back tears of frustration and guilt, I went to bed in the hopes of snatching a little sleep before the next disaster fell on our heads.

The following morning, a cloud of gloom hung over the entire inn. From Mercy's expression, she hadn't slept a lot either, and none of us spoke much at breakfast. With the exception of my parents, of course, who happily discussed their latest hat ideas over the table. Since I was happy to cling to one semblance of normality, I left them to it. As for their offer to let us sell some of their antlers at the inn, that would have to wait until we were rid of our reptilian guests in the hall.

After my parents had returned to their room to get ready for the day, Mercy and I turned to the task we'd been putting off the previous day: dismantling the remnants of our weekend event.

"We might as well start processing the refunds for the play tickets, for a start," she said. "We need to call the choir too. I couldn't get through to them yesterday, but the event is tomorrow. They deserve to know it's not going ahead."

"And the theatre group?" I asked. "Have you heard from them?"

"I haven't. To be honest, I'm waiting for Marcus to call and boast that he's working with Janice instead."

"Not necessarily. Sounds like someone's been pranking her too. And what about Daryl? Isn't he out of the hospital by now?"

"Not yet, I don't think." She looked down, a flush lighting her cheeks. "I wondered about visiting him, but if Marcus is there, I don't want him to start lecturing me again. Besides, I was thinking..." She trailed off.

"Thinking what?"

She drew in a breath. "What you said about Daryl using the wishing box himself... I've been thinking it over, and he does at least have a motive to have taken it, even if it wasn't him who caused all our misfortune."

"You think he's the one who's had it the whole time?" I highly doubted he'd opted to get himself bitten by a snake in order to impress Mercy, but it wasn't like I had any better ideas.

"I can't think of anyone else who knew about it that early on. Except for us..."

"And except for my sister," I added. "Janice, too, but whoever's using the box has been targeting both of us. Who has a grudge against us both?"

"Not just us and Janice," said Mercy. "The theatre group might have been the targets too. Maybe the person who wrecked the costumes was aiming at them instead. Same with the tinsel."

"Don't forget the choir," I said. "They got hit too."

"I doubt I'll forget anytime soon." She approached the door to the hall, still decorated with my useless banner. "I don't hear any more hissing. It might be safe to check on our tinsel."

"Go ahead." I walked behind her, prepared to intervene if the hall did turn out to still be full of snakes.

Mercy opened the door, approaching the cage of chairs in the corner of the hall. Inside lay a heap of multi-coloured, glittering tinsel, without a single snake in sight. "Finally, some good news."

"Except we're the ones who have to put the decorations back up." I glanced over at the door, seeing my parents had entered the reception area. "It's not going to do much good lying on the floor, though."

Mum entered the hall, spotting the small mountain of tinsel inside the hall. "No more snakes, I take it?"

"Just tinsel." I began moving some of the chairs back into line. "Might take a while to fix everything, but it'll give us something to do."

"We can help," Mum insisted, bounding over to pick up a piece of tinsel. "Just tell us where to put it."

Gratitude flooded me. "Thanks. Um, tell you what, you can put the chairs back in line. I'll deal with the tinsel."

I went to fetch the stepladder before I got to work, recalling an unfortunate incident when Bella and I were kids involving Dad, a collapsed stepladder, and several broken bones. Given our abysmal luck this week, I'd rather be the one to climb the ladder.

I hung up loops of tinsel around the hall and Mercy took care of the tree in the reception area while we waited for the kitchen staff to show up so we could tell them about the cancelled event in person. Mercy's idea, not mine, because I was less than convinced that they'd come back at all after the snake fiasco yesterday.

After a few minutes of hanging decorations up, however, I heard raised voices coming from the entryway. Abandoning the tinsel, I ran out and found the kitchen staff gathering in the lobby, looking at Mercy in bewilderment.

"You mean to tell me you cancelled the event without telling us?" Angus said.

"We had to," she said. "The theatre group quit because of the incident with the snakes."

"Of course that Marcus threw a tantrum," said the chef, rolling his eyes. "Should have known."

"In fairness to him, I might have cancelled an event if

one of my colleagues was bitten by a snake too," I said. "We're still happy to pay for the refreshments. We're coming up with a replacement for tomorrow's event—"

"Then I hope you'll enlighten us on what it is before the event starts," one of the other staff members said in sour tones.

"We will," said Mercy. "Sorry. If it's any consolation, the snakes have all gone, and they won't be coming back."

The staff did not look convinced, and they left for the kitchen without another word.

I winced. "That could have gone better."

"What's the betting they'll be next to quit? I get why they're annoyed at Marcus, but there aren't many people who'd be okay with performing where the decorations keep turning into deadly animals."

Our earlier conversation about Daryl came floating back into my mind. "If Daryl *did* take the wishing box, do you think Marcus knew?"

Mercy's brow furrowed. "How on earth would I know?"

"Someone has to," I said. "Tell you what, we'll list everyone who might've known we had the box. We have to start somewhere."

The two of us resumed hanging tinsel around the tree in the reception area as we talked through our theories so far.

"Okay, what was our first issue?" asked Mercy. "The snowstorm, right?"

"Janice might have used a spell and not the box," I said. "Otherwise... how many people came near the inn within the same day of the wishing box's disappearance?"

"Your family, but you already struck them off the list.

Oh, if Charlie took the box outside into the back yard, anyone might've dropped by and taken it if they knew it was there. I'm not sure who told Daryl, actually."

"Then maybe you should go to visit Daryl in the hospital and ask him in person. He might be willing to confide in you."

Her cheeks reddened at that comment. "I guess it's worth having a word with him, if he's allowed visitors."

The phone rang shrilly, and she hastened to answer. I, meanwhile, checked up on my family to find them lovingly draping tinsel all over the chairs. While I moved to finish putting up the piece I'd abandoned above the stepladder, I ran through a mental list of the rest of the week's incidents which might have been attributed to the wishing box. After the snowstorm, there'd been the mishap with the costumes, but I didn't think one of the theatre group's own members would have been responsible for that. That seemed counterproductive to say the least.

After climbing down the ladder, I returned to find Mercy had put down the phone. "The choir finally got through to us, and they want an explanation."

"What do we tell them?" I asked. "That the event is cancelled? Or should we ask them to sing for our guests anyway?"

She pursed her lips. "They're coming here in an hour. Do you reckon that's enough time for us to slip over to the hospital to see Daryl?"

"I'd say it is, but one of us has to watch the desk."

"I'll do it," someone said.

Both of us looked up at the speaker. Bella had entered, her expression half determined, half apprehensive. At first, I couldn't fathom why she'd possibly want to take on unnecessary work. Then I realised it was a test to see if I trusted her to watch the inn in my absence, after my earlier claims that I did believe she hadn't taken the box.

I nodded. "Sure, you can keep an eye on things. Let me know if anyone needs us."

"Okay." She positioned herself behind the desk while Mercy and I fetched our coats and walked out into the crisp morning air.

Mercy glanced through the closing door at my sister. "You two made it up, then?"

"I hope so," I said. "I apologised for not trusting her, and she tried to convince me to blame her anyway so the event can go ahead. Not sure it would have helped, though."

"No," she said. "Honestly, it's not like we could have told the kitchen staff any earlier than we did without calling them out of work hours. As for the choir, I'm not sure they would have believed me if I told them the issues with our phone were a side effect of the wishing box too."

We reached the hospital and asked to see Daryl, who was close enough to being discharged that the staff let us in without a fuss. I'd half expected to find Marcus in there, but either he didn't like hospitals or he didn't feel it was worth the bother because he was nowhere to be found. Instead, Daryl sat up in bed watching TV and looking positively relaxed. Admittedly, it couldn't be pleasant getting yelled at by Marcus all the time during rehearsals, so it was probably nice for him to get a break from that.

When he saw Mercy, however, he yelped and nearly fell out of bed. "What... what are you two doing here?"

"We came to see you," I said. "How are you doing?"

"Good. I should be able to go home today. Are the snakes still around?"

"No, they turned back into tinsel again," said Mercy. "It's hot in here, isn't it? Let's open a window."

I raised a brow at her—the temperature in here wasn't exactly toasty—but while I'd thought he'd be willing to confide in Mercy, Daryl got so tongue-tied around her that I figured that perhaps I ought to do the questioning instead.

"I have a question," I said to him. "No judgment. Did you take the wishing box?"

His face turned crimson. "I…"

"Daryl, you can tell me in confidence, but I need to know if it's true," I said. "We're almost certain the wishing box has caused pretty much all the trouble we're dealing with at the moment, including the events which made Marcus cancel the show."

He winced. "I didn't mean for any of that to happen."

"Then what did you do?" I asked. "I promise I won't tell anyone else. I just need to know where the box is now."

He hung his head. "I found the box around the back of the inn, and I thought you'd left it out there by accident, so I took it home for safekeeping. Then… well, I gave it a test run before I took it back to you. I wanted to get Mercy to come outside and meet me, but I didn't know it'd start snowing *inside* the building. And then it wouldn't stop, so I ran off in a panic. I'm sorry."

So it wasn't Janice who caused the snowstorm?

"What happened to the box afterwards?" I asked. "Who has it now?"

"I don't know," he whispered. "I was going to put it back at the first opportunity, but it vanished at some point between the snowstorm and when we all went to the inn for the rehearsal."

"Did you tell anyone you had it?"

He shook his head. "No, but I put it in my bag before I left the inn and headed back to the rehearsal room to meet with Marcus. I didn't check on it for a while, but the next time I looked in my bag, it was gone."

Weird. Who might have guessed he had it? Daryl himself had heard about the wishing box before Mercy had even told *me* she'd ordered it, but it was beyond me to figure out who it might have been. "Are you sure you don't remember seeing anyone else?"

Daryl's expression turned thoughtful. "I did run into Larry and the choir on the way to the rehearsal room."

"Wait, you did?"

Before he could say another word, however, Mercy walked over to us, her phone in her hand.

"The choir is back at the inn. We need to talk to them now."

14

Mercy and I all but ran back to the inn from the hospital, so fast that I didn't have the breath to spare to tell her what I'd learned from questioning Daryl. At the inn, several members of the choir had already gathered in the entryway, wielding their usual jingling bells and singing a verse of "O Christmas Tree." At least none of them showed any signs of turning into frogs again, but Bella's disgruntled expression from behind the desk told me she wasn't best pleased with their arrival. When they noticed the pair of us enter, their singing abruptly halted.

"Hey," Mercy said breathlessly. "Sorry, I was running an errand. You're early."

"I couldn't reach you on the phone, so I thought this would be easier," Larry said. "Where were you?"

"Ah, we were visiting Daryl from the theatre group in the hospital," Mercy said. "We've been having issues with our phone all week."

"Daryl got bitten by a snake, right?" asked Larry. "At the rehearsal. How'd that happen?"

"Someone turned all the tinsel inside the inn into snakes." I scanned the carollers, wondering if any of them knew more than they'd let on. Someone had taken the box from Daryl when his back was turned, and he *had* mentioned running into the choir on his way to meet Marcus.

"Was it the same person who turned us into frogs?" Larry asked. "Did you ever find out who was responsible?"

Not exactly. It hadn't been Daryl, though. He'd only wanted to use the box to ask Mercy out, not to play pranks on the choir. Unless that part had been an accidental side effect, of course.

"Not yet," I said carefully. "The snakes turned back into tinsel, just like the frog incident. No lasting harm done."

Aside from the departure of the theatre group, of course, but from Larry's grumpy expression, the odds of us convincing the choir to take the place of the actors were depressingly low. It'd take a miracle just to convince them to sing.

"I heard you cancelled the event," Larry said.

Ah. "Who told you that?"

"The theatre company. We ran into each other at the rehearsal studio."

"You did?" I asked. "Marcus dropped out of the event and dragged the rest of the group along with him, and we've yet to find an alternative. Said he couldn't risk a repeat of the snake incident."

Larry made a sceptical noise. "More like it's because he

got offered a major role in that West End production in London."

Mercy and I exchanged surprised glances. *He did what?*

"How do you know?" I asked.

"I overheard him boasting in the rehearsal studio. Personally, I'll be glad when we're not sharing the same space. His theatre group is always taking over the hall for rehearsals whenever we need it for ourselves. I've heard them making fun of our singing too."

"You two know each other?" That was news to me, but Daryl's earlier comment about running into the choir right before the wishing box's disappearance took on a whole new meaning. Especially since it'd been shortly afterwards that the mishap with the reindeer costumes had taken place. Suspicion filtered in as I looked around at the costumed carollers once again.

"Yeah," said Larry. "Wish I didn't know him, personally."

"When was the last time you saw Daryl?" I asked.

"Daryl?" he echoed. "He's still in the hospital, right?"

"Yes, but he said he ran into the choir outside the rehearsal studio other day." My gaze slid across the choir's members. "At the time, he was carrying something fairly valuable which went missing not long after."

Most of their group looked confused, but Larry flushed as I looked directly at him. "Something valuable?"

"Yes. Did you take the wishing box from Daryl and turn the theatre group's costumes from reindeer into rabbits?"

All eyes turned to him, including Mercy's and Bella's. A moment of silence passed while Larry's flush deepened.

"Seriously?" asked Mercy.

"Oh, come on, it was funny," he said defensively. "I didn't know he'd be such a drama queen about it."

I stared disbelievingly at Larry. "What happened to the box, then? Because Mercy and I were the ones who ordered the wishing box to use at our event, but we haven't seen it since before Daryl got hold of it."

Alarm flickered across the elf's features. "I thought the wishing box belonged to Daryl. When we ran into one another, I heard him boasting about how he was going to use it to ask you out, Mercy."

Daryl sure didn't mention that part. Too embarrassed, I guessed. "So you stole it?"

"I borrowed it to mess with him," he mumbled. "I thought it belonged to him."

"No, it was ours," I said. "Mercy's, technically, since she's the one who paid for it. What did you do with it, then?"

"I put it back… or I thought I did," he said. "I left it in the theatre group's changing room at the rehearsal studio. Figured I made a mistake when we all ended up turning into frogs, but of course, it'd long since disappeared by the time I got back to the rehearsal studio again."

"Daryl wouldn't have turned you into frogs," Mercy said promptly.

"Someone did," he said.

No wonder the choir hadn't been fazed over the frog incident, if Larry had assumed it was a one-off caused by someone they knew. But that didn't seem to be the case at all.

"So the frog spell was caused by someone in the theatre group," I said. "The snakes, though? That can't have been them."

And what about Janice's complaints about someone flooding her inn and pranking her? If she'd been telling the truth, the question remained open as to who'd target her as well as Mercy and me. I was pretty sure she'd never exchanged two words with the carollers. As for the theatre group? I needed to talk to Marcus again, but the odds of him being cooperative were lower than those of a heat wave at Santa's palace. Especially if he'd supposedly been offered a major role in London.

Something was fishy there, that was for sure.

"I don't know who turned your tinsel into snakes," Larry said. "None of us did. The box was out of my hands, and nobody else in our group used it, as far as I'm aware."

"Okay," I said. "I need to have a word with Marcus. Are you all absolutely certain that none of you has seen the box recently?"

"Positive," Larry said promptly. "So Daryl stole the box from you? Is that what you're saying?"

"He borrowed it," I corrected him. "With the intention of returning it to us, which went up in the air when you took it from *him.* If we don't get it back before the weekend, our event is over."

"Also, those costumes caused us no end of hassle," Mercy added. "Do you have any idea how long it took me to get through to the online company on the phone? I couldn't get a refund because the site kept crashing and the staff were being unhelpful. I suppose that was a side effect of the wishing box's spell too."

He flushed again. "I didn't realise it'd go that far, I swear."

Mercy gave him a blistering look. "If you *were* responsible for the snakes, you nearly got someone seriously hurt."

"No…" Larry faltered. "I didn't. Nothing I put into the box could possibly have that side effect."

"It doesn't sound like it's possible to have total control over what the box does, though," I said. "If you make a wish, the box seems to go out of its way to make it come true by influencing events by any means possible."

Like causing websites to crash, phones to disconnect… and events to be cancelled. And lives to be placed in dire peril, maybe. If the person who'd caused the snake incident hadn't done so intentionally, then we'd have to have a serious debate over whether to use the box ourselves at all.

At that moment, the group of carollers shuffled away from the door, revealing Janice elbowing her way into the inn. "You think you're being funny, do you?"

"What are you talking about?" I asked.

"You wrecked my sledge!" she said. "A block of ice fell out of the sky and crushed it!"

"I didn't do anything." I glanced at Mercy, who looked as bewildered as I felt. "We went to visit Daryl in the hospital, and then we came straight back here to talk to the choir."

She snorted. "A likely story."

"It's true," I said. "You know that missing wishing box I mentioned? Turns out that Daryl was the one who caused the blizzard, while the carollers were behind the incident with the costumes."

"Am I supposed to feel sorry for you?" Janice wanted to know.

"What my sister is trying to say," said Bella, "is that

she's sorry for accusing you of stealing the box and using it against her."

A flush crept up my neck. "Yeah, pretty much."

Janice made a sceptical noise. "I'll believe that when I see it. You still haven't denied wrecking my sledge."

"I didn't even know you had a sledge," I said. "I *did* have a wishing box, which several people here can attest to. I can also prove it was stolen by someone who'd have good reason to turn us against one another."

"And who might that be?"

Behind the counter, the phone rang. Loudly. Mercy grabbed it then held it out towards me. "Someone's on the phone for you, Carol."

I glanced at Janice. "Bear with me. I have to take this."

"Of course you do." She shoved her way through the carollers to the door as I took the phone from Mercy, already knowing who I'd find on the other end.

Marcus. The person who'd complained the most about the weekend's events being derailed couldn't be the culprit, or so I'd thought. Someone in his own group had got bitten, after all, though it'd explain why he hadn't visited Daryl in the hospital. Yet I was out of any better ideas.

I gripped the phone in my hand. "What is it, Marcus?"

"The last tickets for tomorrow's event are gone," he said. "We're officially sold out."

"I thought you already quit." I glanced at Mercy, who raised her brows in a non-committal manner. "The snakes have gone, if it helps."

"The rest of the group is willing to go ahead with the show, snakes or no snakes. Even Daryl. I'd rather discuss it in person, though."

What was he playing at? Apprehension dug its heels in, and I hesitated before saying, "The choir is here at the moment, but I'll let you know when they're gone."

"I'm at the theatre rehearsal space. Can you spare half an hour to drop by?"

I glanced around at the others, then my gaze landed on Mercy. The last time the wishing box had been seen had been at the rehearsal studio. If Marcus wanted to talk in person, then so be it.

Time to settle this once and for all.

15

Janice had disappeared by the time I hung up, while the choir crowded around the desk, asking questions.

"I won't be long," I told them. "I'm going to speak to Marcus."

"Are you sure?" asked Mercy. "What does he want to tell you that he can't say over the phone?"

"He said some of the theatre group might be willing to go ahead with the show even with the risk of something else going wrong. Besides, the rehearsal studio is the last place the box was seen. It's worth another look around."

From Mercy's expression, she'd guessed my theory, but also guessed that I didn't want the whole world to know. Not until I had more proof, anyway. After the mistake I'd made with Janice, I needed to tread carefully this time.

I didn't think going to the studio alone was my best idea either, but it was that or risk the theatre company and the choir getting into a brawl with one another once the truth got out about Larry's stunt with the costumes. No, I was better off talking to Marcus by myself before figuring out my next move.

I walked across town to the rehearsal studio, which both the theatre group and the choir used to practise in. The plain building might well be the only place in town bare of Christmas decorations, possibly because Marcus had insisted on minimalist décor to avoid distracting his fellow actors. Or because he was the most joyless person at the North Pole. Whatever the case, I found the inside was as bare as the outside. The rest of the group must have gone home for the day because all I found was a deserted corridor leading into a wooden-floored room where Marcus stood alone, waiting for me.

"You came," he said, apparently unaware of how much he sounded like a Bond villain. Or maybe it was intentional. You never knew.

"I saw Daryl in the hospital earlier." Lying, I added, "He seemed upset that you never went to visit him."

"We have a busy schedule," he said, with no emotion whatsoever in his voice.

"Yeah, it looks that way." I indicated the empty room.

His eyes narrowed a little at my sarcasm. "Daryl will be fine. I heard he's out of the hospital now, anyway."

"He had a lucky escape. Considering he got bitten by a snake because someone used a wishing box to wreck our rehearsal without any care for the potential side effects."

"A wishing box?" he echoed.

"Yes, the one Mercy and I ordered to use at our weekend event. Daryl borrowed it from us, and then Larry had it for a bit, after which he left it in your dressing room."

"Larry?" A muscle ticked in his jaw. "What did *he* do with the box, I wonder?"

"What he did with it was fairly harmless compared to turning the tinsel into snakes. Or turning the choir into frogs and playing cruel pranks on Janice with the intention of her blaming me for them. I'd like to know who *currently* has it."

He took a step closer to me. "What are you implying?"

"I want the wishing box back," I said, "and I think it's somewhere in here."

Marcus shook his head. "Janice says you're losing your grip, and I'm inclined to agree with her."

I raised a brow. "I take it she doesn't suspect you're the one who made it rain inside her inn and dropped a block of snow on her sledge, among other things?"

He blinked, not missing a beat, ever the expert actor. "Excuse me?"

"She thought I was responsible," I went on. "Which was probably the point, I imagine, because I thought *she* was the one playing tricks on me."

"Yes, you did," he said. "You told me."

"And *you* decided to tell tales on me to her. This is about more than just your feud with Larry and the choir, isn't it?"

"Larry humiliated me," he said. "I had to see to it that he never did it again."

"You could have stopped there." Now the gloves were coming off. I could hardly believe he'd had the nerve to turn the entire choir into frogs due to a grudge against a single person and then blatantly lie to my face the way he had. "You could have just given me the box back, and I wouldn't have known you were the culprit."

"That's right, you wouldn't have. You're just like that ridiculous family of yours. The moment I set eyes on them, I realised we made a grave error in agreeing to work for you. I deserve far greater things."

"You *what?*" Anger spiked inside me. "Don't you even think about blaming my family for this. They didn't do anything to you. Nor did any of the other people you targeted. Besides, you volunteered to take part in our production this weekend. You didn't have to."

"Back then, I had little choice," he said. "Now I have the box, I can get anything I ask for."

Finally, he'd openly admitted he had it. "What do you want, then?"

"Everything," he said. "I can get out of this town and travel the world. I will become the best actor in a generation. Everyone will know my name."

So that was his plan. Everything had been a means to an end, and the rest of us had simply been obstacles in the way of his pursuit of his ambitions.

"You put one of your own people in the hospital, in case you've forgotten," I said. "You ruined Janice's week as well as mine, and you could have got someone seriously hurt. You didn't even have to stay in town if you wanted to leave so badly."

"The theatre group is completely broke," he said. "We needed a miracle for any of us to get anywhere at all… and I was just lucky that one landed in my lap."

My mouth fell open. "You *stole* it. You think I'm just going to let you fly off with the wishing box and leave the rest of us in the dust?"

"Yes. Oh, I know you don't intend to let me leave

without stopping me… so I saw to it that you won't stand in my way."

My heart gave a jolt. I tried to speak, except no sound came out. When I attempted to take a step forward, my body remained frozen in place. Had he used a spell on me? He hadn't moved… but he hadn't needed to.

"Good." He looked me up and down with a self-satisfied expression. "I got the wording right. The box took me a few attempts to master, but I believe I'm adept enough to use it for what I need."

I could hardly believe his nerve, even if his arrogance wasn't entirely a surprise. He'd effectively stopped me in my tracks, and for all I knew, he'd leave me here for the duration in order to make sure I never tried to get in the way of his ambitions. Then we'd all lose our chance to make sure he was punished justly for all the trouble he'd caused.

The door rattled behind me. I would have jumped, but my body remained locked to the spot, and I couldn't move an inch.

"Carolyn, are you okay?" Mum called through the door.

They followed me again. I tried to speak, but once again, no sound came out. The door rattled again, yet it didn't open. Another effect of the wishing box, no doubt.

"She'll go away soon enough," Marcus said in a low voice.

She won't. My parents were as stubborn as I was, and even with the wishing box in his possession, he couldn't have foreseen every single eventuality. Even *I* hadn't known my parents had followed me here.

Too bad there wasn't anything I could do as long as the

box's spell held me in its grip. Sweat trickled down my neck as I fought the invisible force holding me in place and the door rattled in its frame over and over. The box's magic was powerful, but it must have a limit somewhere, surely. If I could just *think...*

A soft thudding sounded from the corridor. Marcus's eyes narrowed. "What are you doing?"

Me? Nothing. I still couldn't speak, but my heart lifted when Charlie the cat appeared in the corner of my eye. It seemed the box's effects hadn't spread to him. Or maybe it didn't affect cats. A glint caught the light, and my heart flipped over as I realised the cat held the gleaming red box in his mouth. I remained still, but Marcus had seen my reaction, however muted, and his gaze landed on the cat as he streaked towards the back door.

"Give me that box!" he shouted.

He ran after the cat, but Charlie had swiftly discovered the back door was locked too. Veering to the side, the cat pelted through Marcus's legs and tripped him up in the process.

Marcus went down, hard, at the same time as the front door opened and revealed my parents. Mum held out her arms for Charlie to run up to her and took the box from his mouth. "Oh, is that it? Excellent."

Marcus stumbled upright, but faster than I'd ever have thought possible, Mum opened the box and put a scrap of paper inside it.

At once, the frozen sensation left me, and I could move again. I started to cross the room to my parents, only for Marcus to bar my path.

"If I can't use the box, I'll have to restrain you myself."

I tensed, and a flash of light engulfed the room. My

eyes screwed up instinctively, and when I blinked the glare away, nothing more than a single rat lay in Marcus's place.

The rat squealed as Charlie bore down on him and pinned him to the spot with a paw.

"Don't eat him!" I warned.

"Oops." Mum eyed the box in her hands. "That box *is* a little over the top, isn't it?"

"You might say that." I walked over to Charlie's side, keeping an eye on the squirming rat. "How'd you even know he had the box?"

"Bella and Mercy told us everything they knew," Dad said. "Why did you come here alone?"

"Because—" I cut myself off. "I wanted to get a confession from him without anyone else getting involved, but that wasn't my smartest idea. Nobody else even heard him confess."

"I beg to differ," said a voice from behind Mum and Dad. Janice walked into view, eyeing Marcus's rat-form. "It was *you* who was playing tricks on me, and you wanted me to blame Carol for it."

"So I'd be too busy arguing with you to notice that he was the one who took the box," I added. "He must have guessed I figured it out when I visited Daryl in the hospital. Daryl was the first person who took the box, and it changed hands a couple of times before Marcus snatched it up. Did you hear the part when he told me he planned to fly off to act in a play in the West End?"

"He *what?*" another voice rang out from behind my parents.

The two of them moved aside as several other members of the theatre group crowded into the doorway.

With the door open, they'd heard every word of our confrontation, and they eyed Marcus the rat with expressions of shock and betrayal on their faces. Even Daryl had shown up. He must have run straight here to join the others as soon as he'd been discharged from the hospital.

"You were the one who ruined our rehearsal?" Daryl asked Marcus. "And caused me to get bitten by a snake?"

"Yes," I said. "He pranked the choir too. And Janice."

"I knew he was a rat." Mercy walked in, her phone in her hand. "I'll call the police, but I think they'll only be able to arrest him if he's human."

"We'll keep him as a rat until they get here." While Mercy called the police, I watched him to make sure he didn't try to make a quick getaway. Not that he could do anything as a rat.

Meanwhile, Mum handed me the wishing box back, along with a notebook and pen, but I hesitated before writing anything down. The box had caused so many mishaps, even if most of them were down to Marcus's meddling. I'd need to think carefully about the wording.

I wrote down, *I wish Marcus would turn human again as soon as the police have him cornered.*

After double-checking my words for ambiguity, I placed the note into the box.

The police showed up within a few minutes, at which point Marcus transformed into a human again. They had him cuffed within seconds, and his protests fell on deaf ears as they hauled him away. With him gone, quietness descended on the room, interspersed with admiring murmurs fixated on the box in my hands.

"Nobody else is going to use the box," Mercy said, raising her voice so that everyone in the room could hear.

"Not before we can ensure there won't be a repeat of anything Marcus did."

A murmur of agreement passed through the theatre group.

"We might need a miracle to pull off tomorrow's event," I added, "but I want to offer you the choice of whether or not you want to take part in the show, even without Marcus."

Silence fell again, much tenser than before. Then….

"We're in," said Daryl. "We won't let him ruin the show."

"Agreed," said one of the others, and they all chimed in in unison.

"Thanks." Dizzy relief flooded me as the others agreed with him. "Ah… without Marcus, we have nobody to play the leading reindeer, but we can adjust the script."

"I can do it," said Daryl. "We all know each other's parts. It seems only fair to go through with the event after Marcus tried to abandon us. Right?"

Murmurs and nods followed, and even Janice gave me a nod as though giving me her blessing.

I waited for the others to fall silent before addressing the theatre group again. "Janice has an event next week too. You might want to consider helping her out, since Marcus was giving her trouble as well."

Janice's mouth fell open in shock. She recovered swiftly as the group descended on her to ask her for the details, while I moved back to Mercy's side.

"What do you reckon we should do with the box?" she asked. "Use it to ensure the event goes ahead without any more issues?"

"Honestly?" I said. "I'm not sure we'll need it."

16

As I'd predicted, we didn't need the wishing box for the show to go on as planned, but Mercy and I kept it in reserve. Just in case.

During the performance, my family sat in the front row, and I was in such a good mood that Mum and Dad's over-the-top reactions were endearing rather than annoying. Even Bella managed to refrain from complaining, even as fake snow cascaded from the ceiling and kept landing in her lap. She remained on her best behaviour, though, watching the show without making any derisive comments. I respected her self-control if nothing else, but she'd shown a surprising level of tolerance for the ways of Holiday Haven. In fact, she'd single-handedly sold a dozen of Mum and Dad's newly made reindeer hats to the guests when she'd taken over the reception while Mercy and I ran around making last-minute preparations for the event.

Given the tight time frame, even the wishing box wouldn't have been able to lower our stress, but we'd decided it was best to go through the event without adding any more unnecessary complications. It was a miracle worthy of the box itself that we'd managed to get everything ready in time, not to mention explaining to the choir and the kitchen staff that Marcus was behind most of the issues over the past week and that the event would be taking place after all.

Onstage, the reindeer burst into song with what felt like twice the usual enthusiasm. Without exception, the theatre group were all thrilled that Marcus had been hauled off to jail instead of getting to act in the West End. Daryl in particular seemed to be in an incredibly good mood, though rumour had it that he had a date with Mercy after the show. I'd have to ask her about that later.

In the meantime, the reindeer cavorted offstage as the play stopped for the interlude. As the guests began to rise to their feet, the catering staff led them to the buffet tables laden with snowflake cakes and reindeer cookies. Several of them wore hats they'd purchased from reception—my parents had gone overboard making antlers overnight again—and dozens of antlers bobbed as the crowd milled around the hall, chatting excitedly.

We'd had so many extra requests for tickets that we'd had to bring in extra chairs, and we'd never had so many bookings for new guests, either. Word of Marcus's antics had been the talk of Holiday Haven, and his arrest had occupied the front page of *Hark! The Herald,* but a fair bit of the newfound interest in the inn came from the mystique around the wishing box and the suspense over whether it'd make an appearance today after all.

As the guests began to file out of the hall and into the reception area, Mercy stepped up behind the desk and cleared her throat loudly. "Everyone, can I have your attention for a minute?"

All eyes turned to her, then everyone broke out in spontaneous applause. I ducked through the crowd and joined her behind the desk. Then, the applause petered out when I pulled the wishing box out of its hiding place and held it up to show everyone. "This is our exclusive feature for the day. I'm sure you've all heard about it already."

A murmur passed among the gathering guests—part excitement, part wariness. Having heard the full story, they had good reason to be wary of our new toy.

"The wishing box is strictly for gift-related wishes only," Mercy told them. "Anyone who wants to get the gift of their dreams is welcome to give it a shot. One wish per person. Write out your wish on a piece of paper and hand it to our assistant, who'll give her approval if it's ready to go into the box."

As another murmur went through the crowd, Bella approached from the back room. Mum and Dad had somehow got her into a reindeer hat, which only served to make her scowl even funnier while the guests surged towards the desk to pick up paper and pens to write down their wishes.

"I'm reading every wish before it goes in the box," Bella told them. "Every single one. No funny business."

Some people were bound to try wishing for something ridiculous, of course, but Bella was more than prepared to ensure only the legitimate wishes made it to the box. Leaving her to it, I tracked down my parents beside the tinsel-clad tree, safe in the knowledge that it was not going to turn into snakes at any moment. They wore matching reindeer hats of their own, and both of them beamed when they spotted me.

"You did a great job, Carolyn," said Mum.

"You did," Dad agreed.

My flush deepened when both their hats started singing loudly at me and drew the attention of everyone in the area, but their costumes had helped save the show, so I refrained from asking them to tone it down.

"Are you still going home tomorrow?" I asked.

"We have to get back to the hat shop," Dad said. "We'll have to come back and visit again in nicer weather."

I raised a brow. "You know it always snows here, right?"

"Joking, joking." Dad laughed. "I think Bella is warming to the weather. Get it?"

"Yeah, I get it." I grinned, glancing over at my sister. Bella did seem to have taken to her new position at the front desk, though she probably enjoyed using her authority to approve or reject people's requests for the wishing box more.

Mercy, too, was back to her usual cheerful self as she chatted with the guests. The carollers, meanwhile, entered for the interlude and broke into song loud enough to drown out both my parents' hats. I even spotted Janice lurking near the back, though she disappeared before I had the chance to talk to her. Maybe she was embarrassed about how I'd given the theatre group the go-ahead to work at her event too. Or maybe she was fishing for ideas to 'borrow.' I didn't mind either way.

The show went on, and the Holiday Haven Inn was open for business.

Read all of the
Winter Witches of Holiday Haven

SLEIGH SPELLS — BELLA FALLS

REINDEER RUNES — DANIELLE GARRETT

HOLIDAY HEXES — J. L. COLLINS

WINTER WISHES — ELLE ADAMS

COCOA CURSES — ERIN JOHNSON

WWW.WINTERWITCHESBOOKS.COM

ABOUT THE AUTHOR

Elle Adams lives in the middle of England, where she spends most of her time reading an ever-growing mountain of books, planning her next adventure, or writing. Elle's books are humorous mysteries with a paranormal twist, packed with magical mayhem.

She also writes urban and contemporary fantasy novels as Emma L. Adams.

Find Elle on Facebook at https://www.facebook.com/pg/ElleAdamsAuthor/

Or sign up to her newsletter at:
smarturl.it/ElleAdamsNewsletter

Printed in Poland
by Amazon Fulfillment
Poland Sp. z o.o., Wrocław